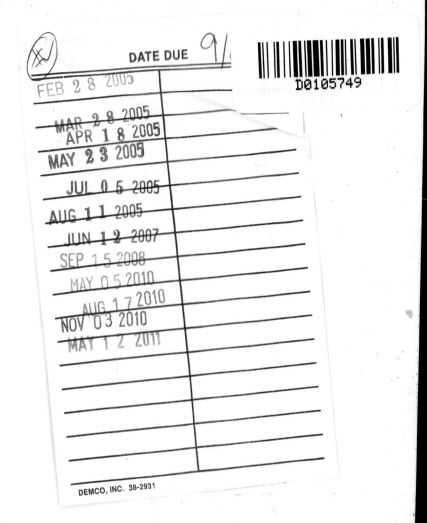

Melinda Metz

HarperCollins*Publishers*

www.harperchildrens.com

Library of Congress Cataloging-in-Publication Data
Metz, Melinda.
   Raven's Point / by Melinda Metz.— 1st ed.
     p.   cm.
   Summary: An ancient evil has reawakened on a small island off the
coast of Rhode Island, eager to cause death and destruction as it has
twice before, but three teens face it with their newly developed super-
natural abilities.
   ISBN 0-06-052371-9 — ISBN 0-06-052372-7 (lib. bdg.)
   [1. Supernatural—Fiction.   2. Time travel—Fiction.   3. Ghosts—
Fiction.   4. Human-animal communication—Fiction.   5. Islands—
Rhode Island—Fiction.   6. Rhode Island—Fiction.]   I. Title.
PZ7.M5673Rav   2004   2003022880
[Fic]—dc22

Typography by Rob Hult
1 2 3 4 5 6 7 8 9 10
❖
First Edition

For my parents, Richard and Jan Metz, who have supported me and my writing in every possible way—research, compliments, air-conditioning, nationwide word-of-mouth advertising campaigns, cash, and love.

Small. Thin. No bones. No claws. No teeth. No
poison. Just softness. Weakness. But I am alive.
They think me dead, they think they killed me,
but I live.

Dark earth surrounds me. Presses down on me.
Hides me. The darkness is my whole world. I
know the sun still shines only because there are
times when I feel a hint of its warmth.

One day I will see the sun again. I will rest. I will
grow strong. I will emerge into the light.

One day I will be mightier than the sun. And my
enemies will burn.

And this time they will die forever.

Chapter 1

A Beautiful Day
in the Neighborhood

Jane Romano ran the comb through her big brother's light brown hair one final time. She could feel the heat of his scalp beneath her fingers. The heat always freaked her out. She kept expecting Elijah to feel cold. Not dead cold, god no. More like refrigerated-to-keep-you-fresh cold.

Stop thinking about him like he's a carton of leftover Chinese or something, Jane ordered herself. She dropped the comb on the nightstand next to the yellow plastic pitcher. She was thirsty, but she didn't pour water into one of the plastic cups.

It was ridiculous, she knew that, but she had this cave-person primal fear that if she ate or drank anything in Elijah's room she would slip into a coma too, and spend the rest of her life lying in the bed next to his. "Oh, the Romano children," people would say. "So sad. So tragic. Their poor parents. But at least they look peaceful."

Jane swallowed, trying to bring some moisture to her dry throat, and forced a smile, even though, duh, Elijah couldn't see her. "Ready for the report from the invisible girl of Raven's Point High?" she asked.

She hesitated. The best gossip du jour was that Tavia Burrows had finally hooked up with Thomas Bledsoe. But her brother probably wouldn't want to hear that his girlfriend, make that his first love—not that Elijah would use those words—had moved on. Jane searched her brain for blander school news.

"Okay, I was in the bathroom at school," Jane began, "and Andrea Callison was complaining to her sidekick, Madeline, that nothing she'd tried had gotten any attention from Seth oh-my-God-that-boy-is-hot McFadden. That was Andrea saying Seth's hot, not me. Although, Jesus please-us, is he. Not that he would ever look at a sophomore. Any sophomore. Especially one who—"

Jane gave her head an impatient shake. "What am I doing? We're talking about Andrea here. She actually tried wearing nippies to get Seth to take a second look. What, you might ask, if you weren't in a coma, are nippies? Well, I'll tell you. They are fake nipples. You wear them to make it look like you're, uh, interested, or I guess cold, all the time."

Jane sucked in a breath. Could Elijah hear her from someplace deep in the center of his brain? And if he could, was she torturing him by giving him these total fluff reports about high school? He'd be a senior now. Was she just reminding him of everything he was missing? Or if he could talk, would he tell her to read him the paper or give him the update on their parents, anything but mindless gab-gab about people he hadn't even cared about when he was conscious?

Stop making yourself crazy, Jane thought. "When I leave I'll turn on CNN," she promised her brother. "What was I saying? Oh, yeah. Andrea and her Seth safari. So—"

"I was expecting your dad," Mrs. Callison said from the doorway.

Mrs. Callison, mother of Andrea Callison. How much had she heard? Had she heard about the nippies? This was what happened when you lived in a small town—on an island—where everybody knew everybody.

Don't go into a meltdown, Jane ordered herself. Answer the woman. "Yeah, Dad usually does the morning visit, but I was up early so I told him I'd come today."

Which sort of pissed Mom off, Jane added silently. Because Mom didn't want anyone to visit Elijah. No, that wasn't true. She just didn't want Jane's dad to visit every day. She didn't think it was healthy. But Jane knew not visiting would drive her dad nuts, which was why she was sitting in the hospital at the ungodly hour of—she checked the clock—six-twenty. Her being there would make her dad feel better. Although it wouldn't keep her mother from being pissed off. Although she was less pissed off than if Jane's dad had come.

Dealing with her parents was like doing a chemistry experiment that could explode and singe off your eyebrows at any second. Jane tried to keep everything balanced, but even though most days she managed to avoid a ka-boom, she never came up with exactly the right formula to keep both parents happy. Just thinking about it made the muscles in her jaw clench, her teeth squeaking against each other.

Mrs. Callison checked the level on one of the two bags that was dripping some kind of liquid food into Elijah. "Tell your dad that last night Muffin, the therapy dog, came to visit. He hopped right up on Elijah's bed and stayed there for half an hour. That dog's coat is so glossy. I wish my hair looked that good." Mrs. Callison replaced one of the bags with a fresh one. "Do you want anything, Jane? Juice? Or I brought in some banana-nut muffins."

Mrs. Callison tried to be everybody's mom. "No thanks," Jane answered. Mrs. Callison gave a little wave as she left the room.

Jane checked the clock again. She could stay another half hour. "Okay, so, again, what was I saying?" She couldn't remember. Her brain was full of her parents' A.M. fight. *"Every day it's less likely that he'll come out of it. That's what the doctors told us. It's been more than a year. It's over, Brian. Accept it."* Jane's mother's voice had gotten higher and higher with each sentence. The words "accept it" had come out in a screech.

While her father's voice had gotten quieter and quieter. *"I have to keep hoping. I won't survive if I don't. You ask me to accept it. That's the same as asking me to die. Is that what you want, Eleanor?"*

Jane took her brother's hand, something she'd stopped doing when she was a little girl. The heavy, warm weight of it felt good. She had a flash of that same hand on the steering wheel of the old Caddy. Dad had insisted Elijah's first car be big as a tank. He'd thought that would keep Elijah safe.

They'd just been going to the store. Only a few blocks. Elijah had been driving with one hand on the wheel, showing off. Not that it would have changed anything if he'd been using both.

Jane closed her eyes and pulled in a long, slow breath. "Don't think about it," she whispered. She let the breath out, slowly, slowly. She had an algebra test first period. She didn't need to walk into it all freaked. "Don't think about it." Jane pulled in another breath—and the sweet tang of cigar smoke filled her nose and snaked its way down into her lungs.

The fine hairs on Jane's arms stood up. That smell. It shouldn't be here. Not in the hospital. But it was. She could taste it on her tongue. Rich, sharp. Like that day in the car. The windows were rolled up and the smell of cigar smoke from the old guy who used to own the Caddy was really strong.

Just open your eyes, and you'll see that you're sitting in Elijah's hospital room, Jane told herself. But she squeezed her eyes even more tightly closed. She was afraid of what she'd find if she opened them. Because it wasn't just the smell.

There wasn't hard plastic beneath her butt anymore. Now there was something softer than plastic. Something that had been mashed down by lots of butts before hers. The car. She'd been there in her dreams. But she wasn't asleep now. And the Caddy had been junked after the accident, squished into a piece of metal the size of a tin can. So open your eyes, you idiot, Jane ordered herself.

She forced her eyes open and screamed. But the two people in the front seat of the Caddy—Sherman, that's what they'd called it, Sherman for Sherman tank—didn't glance back at her.

"I don't even need one hand," the guy driving said. "I bet I could drive with a finger. Just a pinky. Wanna see?"

Jane hadn't heard that voice for more than a year, but it was so familiar. "Elijah," she whispered. Her brother didn't turn around.

"Elijah." Wait. It was her voice, but she hadn't spoken that time.

It's me up there, she realized. Freshman me with the bad hair and—

"Elijah, green light," the younger Jane prodded.

Elijah pulled out into the intersection. Meridian and Lansford. The Safeway just half a block away.

Jane whipped her head to the left. The SUV was speeding toward them, the driver so wasted he didn't even brake. The squealing brakes might have—

"Elijah, no!" Jane cried. She reached out and grabbed her brother's shoulders. Her fingers slipped right through his flesh.

The SUV slammed into Elijah's door. The Caddy flipped. Jane's world flipped. Then went black.

"Elijaaaah!"

Color flooded back into the world. Yellow pitcher. Patchwork quilt. Peach walls.

Jane heard footsteps rushing toward her. Then Mrs. Callison had her by the arm. "What happened? Are you okay?"

"I was . . ." Jane rubbed her arm, the arm she'd broken in the accident, healed months and months and months ago. "I saw Elijah," she continued. "It was real."

Mrs. Callison turned toward the bed. "Oh, my god. He's awake. Elijah, you're awake!"

Tavia Burrows grabbed a bottle of water out of the freezer. It would be ready to drink when she made it to the top of the point. She snagged her Walkman and double-checked to make sure her *NSYNC CD was in place. For some reason, embarrassing as it was to admit—so embarrassing that she never would admit it—the *NSYNC guys helped her keep moving. She opened the door, then turned around and tossed her Walkman in the junk drawer. She'd forgotten she was running with Thomas.

Suddenly her sports bra felt a little . . . little. And her sweats felt kind of grungy. Should she change or— This is about running, she told herself. Why did it feel so weird running with a guy? Intimate. More intimate than making out. It was all about breathing and sweating and reaching inside to find the iron to go on.

Maybe it's because you used to make this run with Elijah, a little voice in her head whispered. Tavia didn't want to hear it. Elijah was in the past. It had taken her a full year to put him there, and that's where he was going to stay. She had college applications to fill out, SATs to take, meets to win, a life to live. She couldn't afford distractions.

Tavia stepped outside and quietly closed the door behind her. The ocean fog hadn't burned off yet. It was her favorite time to run, the fog embracing her, half blinding her. She stretched her calves and hamstrings, did a few ankle twirls, then started to jog toward Elijah's house.

What was she doing? This was completely the wrong direction. Tavia stopped, pulled in a deep breath, and turned around. She took off toward Thomas's—Thomas's, Thomas's, Thomas's—at an all-out run, as if the fog had turned into ghostly hands running over her body. Elijah's hands. She didn't slow down until she hit Thomas's front yard.

He was waiting for her. He reached for her, and she didn't realize he was planning to kiss her quite fast enough, so he ended up only catching the corner of her mouth. Tavia hadn't thought they were at the casual kiss-hello stage yet. Although last night things had gotten pretty hot between them. But that was different, at the end of a date, at night, just different.

Out of the corner of her eye, Tavia caught a flash of movement in the kitchen window of Thomas's house. Thomas's mom saw that kiss, she realized. Wonder if she's as happy as my mother is that Thomas and I've hooked up. Tavia's mom had always been a little weird about Tavia and Elijah going out. Which made no sense, since Tavia's mother had married a white guy, happily married and still married. Her mom had never said anything about Thomas being African American—one of the few on the island—but Tavia could tell she approved.

"I want to keep moving." Tavia stepped away from Thomas. "I'm already warmed up."

"And I was just starting to get warm," Thomas teased. But he fell in beside Tavia as she jogged down his street, heading for the point. Tavia kept her speed down until she figured Thomas's muscles were loosened up, then lengthened her stride. Almost immediately, she heard a change in Thomas's breathing. He had a light wheeze going. Her legs were itching to really fly, but Tavia forced herself to keep the pace steady. Thomas's wheezing grew louder as they neared the trail that led up the hill.

"Sorry," Thomas said, sounding breathless. "I told you it's been a while since I did any running."

"It's okay. This is just supposed to be for fun," Tavia answered. Although the fun for her was always pushing it, finding the limit, and then going farther.

"It's not going to be that fun waiting for the ambulance when I pass out on the hill." Thomas sucked in a raspy breath.

"So we'll turn around," Tavia said.

"No, you've got to get in your miles before the meet. I'll go back though. I want to be alive to cheer you on." Thomas gave her shoulder a friendly nudge as she passed him. Tavia broke into a sprint. Her calf muscles burned as she headed up to the point. The steep incline never got easier. Her speed got faster, yes. But this part of the run always got her heart pounding and set her lungs on fire.

Tavia reached out and touched the trunk of the huge oak tree at the tip of the point. She caught a glimpse of the ocean slamming into the rocks below—you couldn't go too far on the island without seeing the ocean, although it was still too foggy to see the coastline of Rhode Island. Then she spun around and started back down. Her toes hit the front of her Adidas with each step, and she could feel the pressure in her knees. She didn't care. No minor physical complaints could compare with the rush of flying down the hill, almost losing control. Almost.

When she reached the bottom, Tavia pulled her water out of her pack. She took a swig—little slivers of ice hard against her tongue—pressed a button on the stopwatch around her neck, jammed the bottle back in place, and started up the hill again. Come on, she thought. Today's the day you break it.

"Faster," she said aloud. "Come on. Come on."

Tavia heard footsteps on the dirt behind her. She glanced over her shoulder and saw two dogs. They looked friendly enough—tails up, no teeth showing—so she kept on running.

"Come on, faster. Faster, faster, come on," she muttered.

The bushes ahead of her trembled. A moment later, a white cat with three black paws streaked onto the path. It kept pace with Tavia as she ran. The dogs behind her started to bark. How can two dogs make so much noise? Tavia thought. She shot another look behind her, and her heart slammed up into her throat. There were five dogs now—a dachshund struggling to keep up with the others.

Freaky. That's all, freaky. Don't make an international incident out of it, Tavia told herself. She faced forward again, her stride faltering. A skunk scrambled out of the brush and ran alongside the cat. And in the trees, three squirrels jumped from branch to branch, matching her pace.

Tavia skidded to a stop. The cat froze, except for its tail, which whipped back and forth. The skunk paused in mid-stride, one paw off the ground. The squirrels sat in a row on one tree branch.

This wasn't freaky. It was wrong. Unnatural. Tavia didn't look behind her. She could hear that the dogs had stopped too. But she didn't want to see them.

Just look, she ordered herself. Maybe there's a reason they were all running up the hill. A natural reason. A brush fire or something. Except then why had they stopped? Tavia ignored that last thought. She turned completely around. The dogs, all motionless, stared at her. It seemed like they were waiting . . . for her.

Tavia's eyes darted back and forth, searching for something, anything, that could give her a logical explanation. But there was no smoke. No grizzly bear—not that there had ever been a grizzly bear on Raven's Point. No hunter.

"What?" Tavia burst out. "What do you want?"

Of course there was no answer. That would be insane. Tavia believed in rational explanations, even if you couldn't see them. Animals were supposed to know when an earthquake was coming or a storm. Maybe— But every animal was still now. All those eyes locked on Tavia.

"Just go away, all right? Back to whatever you were doing," she cried.

In unison all the dogs calmly turned and trotted back down the hill. Tavia's heart thudded with heavy, painful beats.

Finish your run, she told herself. Make your miles. By the time she managed to get her feet pointed back up the hill, the cat, the skunk, and the squirrels had disappeared.

Christ, they've heard already, Seth McFadden thought. He pasted a grin on his face and headed down the hall to the guys clustered around his locker. Only ten minutes since the coach told me, and they know. All of them tryin' to imagine what it feels like to be me. If they knew, they'd—

"Hey, McFadden, you're gonna tell the scout that you won't go to Duke unless I go with you, right?" Chad Williams asked. He ran his fingers over the goatee he'd been attempting to grow for a month.

"Yeah, Williams, you're going to be at the top of his list of demands," Matthew Plett shot back. He spat on the floor. Seth was surprised the saliva didn't start to eat through the speckled linoleum like acid.

"Not at the top top," Chad answered, giving Seth a friendly punch. "I mean, you get a Ferrari, a high-paying, low-hassle job, the chance to service all the babes about campus, *and* I go with you."

The wheels in Seth's brain spun. Usually he had no problem knowing what to say. But he was coming up with nothing, at least nothing that didn't make him sound like an arrogant a-hole. Or some young what-would-Jesus-do bracelet wearer. "Now, fellows," he imagined himself saying, "if you play your best I'm sure the scout will be looking at you as much as me."

"You're letting me be in your shoe commercial, right?" Vince Pullman cut in before Seth could come up with something that was only half moronic. "Just as some loser, former high school basketball player who goes 'nice shoes.' That way I'd get me a check every time it came on. And I'd be good at it. Watch. Watch, McFadden." Seth obediently turned toward Vince. Vince gave him a smile that showed every tooth in his head. Then he pointed down at Seth's size-eleven feet. "Nice shoes!" he said, sounding like that freak announcer on *Conan*. "So?" Vince went on in his regular voice. "Waddya say?"

"Oh, please, pretty please, McFadden, will you let me kiss your smooth pink butt?" Matthew begged, getting down on one knee in front of Seth. He fluttered his eyelashes, playing to the crowd, but his green eyes were cold enough to make your balls want to crawl back inside you.

Seth laughed, hoping it sounded a lot less fake than it did in his head. He always pretended he had no idea Matthew was jealous, always gave him the laugh.

"No, but Andrea Callison will be begging him to kiss hers when she hears he's going to Duke," Chad said. The guy was always there for him—on the court or off.

"Now that's an image that will get me through Action Jackson's lecture on the gold standard." Seth pushed his way over to his locker, dialed in the combo, and opened the door. He grabbed his history book, slammed the door, gave a half salute, and headed toward the can. *At least we're guys*, he thought. *I don't have to worry about someone wanting to "keep me company" in the crapper.*

He sped up as he headed away from the group but didn't allow himself to break into a run. "Nice," Seth muttered when he stepped through the door. The bathroom was empty. He rushed over to the last stall, the one next to the high, narrow window, and locked himself in. His fingers shook as he unzipped his backpack and pulled out a box of blueberry Pop-Tarts. A date was written on the cardboard lid in black marker—9/5/2004. So more than two months since the last time. He'd sworn he'd still be carrying this box around on New Year's Eve and it was still a couple weeks until Thanksgiving. Well, screw it. He needed this. Now.

Seth ripped open the box, yanked out the first silver pouch and tore it open with his teeth. He got half of the first pastry in his mouth with the first bite. Before he had a chance to swallow, he shoved in the rest. The hard, dry crust scraped the roof of his mouth, and when he crammed in half of the second Pop-Tart he gagged for a moment. Then he managed to swallow the lump of half-chewed sweet dough.

No thinking. All motion. He ripped open the second foil package. Got two more Pop-Tarts down. They felt like they were stuck at the base of his throat, but what the hell, number five and six would give them a push.

The stall door swung open. What the—He'd locked it. "Somebody's in here," he said, blocking the door with one hand.

The door shoved against his palm. Whoever was out there was freakishly strong. "I said it's taken."

The metal hinges squealed as the stall door was ripped free. A boy stood there. Couldn't be more than a first-grader. Dirt-brown hair. Dirt-brown eyes. Mole to the left of the nose. "Terry." The name came out of Seth's lips in a cracked whisper.

The boy—Terry—smiled. "Hey, Seth. I thought maybe you'd want me to hold your hair back while you puke. But

I guess you want to eat the bonus pack of tarts first. I'll wait."

Terry freakin' Reingold. Seth shook his head. "No way. You're dead. You've been dead for eleven freakin' years."

Terry leaned against the stall's doorframe. "You should know," he answered. "You killed me."

Andrea has nicer clothes than I do, Vicki Callison thought as she hung one of her daughter's silk blouses in the closet. Not that I need nice clothes. Hospital, home. Home, hospital. Those are the only places I ever go.

"How creepy is it that Elijah's awake?" Vicki heard Madeline Gunderson, one of her daughter's crowd, ask. When you were in Andrea's room you could hear every word spoken in the living room. Some fluke of the heating vents. "I mean, what was happening to him that whole time? Like, did he dream or anything?" Madeline went on.

Vicki continued to listen as she transferred the clothes, still warm from the iron, to the closet.

"My mom's one of Elijah's nurses," Andrea told her friends. "She thinks he could have known everything that was going on in his room."

"Interesting," Lucy Choi, another of Andrea's regulars, not one of Vicki's favorites, commented. "That means he would know Tavia stopped visiting about six months ago."

"I doubt that's all that important to him right now," Madeline said. "If I was him, all I'd be thinking is 'I was in a coma. I can't believe I was in a coma.'"

Andrea snorted. "Don't you remember how he and Tavia were together? They were like freakish twins joined at the lips. They weren't even two people."

"As if you wouldn't want to be Seth McFadden's mutant twin. That black hair, those blue eyes, that tight butt," Lucy commented.

Vicki stopped paying attention to the girls' chatter, trying to remember if she'd noticed boys' butts when she was in high school. She didn't think so. Although she'd definitely become something of a butt woman in her later years.

She pulled a pair of hip-hugging burnt-orange suede pants out of the closet. Yes, definitely much nicer than anything she had. Impulsively, Vicky kicked off her sneaks, slid down her stretch jeans, then pulled on Andrea's pants. The suede was heaven against her skin, so soft. But the zipper wouldn't close.

"I haven't forgotten everything I learned in high school," Vicki muttered. She lay down on the bed, flat on her back, and sucked in her stomach, sucked, sucked. And zipped. And smiled. She could wear her teenage daughter's pants. How cool was that?

Vicki levered herself off the bed and walked over to the full-length mirror on the back of Andrea's door. Yes, she'd zipped the pants. But zipping them had pushed lumps of pasty flesh over the waistband. What had she been thinking putting these on?

Through the vent, she heard Andrea give a long trill of laughter. It was almost as if Andrea could see her. As if Andrea was laughing at her mother's doughy body.

"You know how I got this, don't you, little miss Andrea?" Mrs. Callison whispered, grabbing her roll of belly fat in both hands and digging her fingernails into it. "Having you, that's how. I could still wear clothes like this if it wasn't for you. And you never even said thank you."

Andrea laughed again.

Vicki dug her fingernails deeper into her belly, so deep that rivulets of blood ran down her stomach, staining the waistband of the hip huggers, a red so deep it was almost black.

Chapter 2

Dreamland

Seth strode directly to the breakfast food section of the 7-Eleven and grabbed the closest box of Pop-Tarts. The flavor didn't matter. Then he swung around and headed to the laundry stuff. In seconds, he found what he needed—a laundry marker, indelible ink, the nothing-is-going-to-get-this-sucker-off kind. He carried his two items to the cashier, paid, and returned to the car.

Terry Reingold—Terry freakin' Reingold—was sitting shotgun. Seth didn't say anything to him. Okay, Seth was a recovering bulimic freak. A murderer and a recovering bulimic—and isn't that a girl thing?—freak. But he was not going to add off-his-nut whack job who sees dead people to his list of accomplishments. No thanks. Uh-uh.

"Pen," he muttered. Talking to himself wasn't great, but it was still passably sane. He ripped the laundry marker free of its cardboard and hard plastic wrapper. Then he grabbed the box of Pop-Tarts and wrote the date across the front as big as he possibly could.

"Why bother?" Terry asked. "You know you'll have your nose in that trough before the day is over."

"I carried the other box around for two months. Two—" Crap. He was doing it. He was talking to a dead guy. Not even a dead guy, just some piece of dung his brain had farted out. "You don't even sound like Terry," he muttered. "Terry's a first-grader. You sound like you're my age. Which makes sense, because I'm imagining—"

"I've been following you around for eleven years, nimrod," Terry interrupted. "I know I still have the body of a kid, but that's the only part of me that's still six years old."

"Not having this conversation." Seth turned away from Terry and put the box of tarts in his backpack. Having them there, having them and not opening the box, it made him strong. Proved he was beating this thing. Used to be he couldn't go a day without a scarf and barf. This time it had been more than two friggin' months. That meant something.

Seth started up the family Volvo and headed home. He kept his eyes on the road. Period. His neck started cramping with the effort of not looking over at the passenger seat to see if Terry—the thing—had disappeared.

He pulled into the driveway and saw his mother standing there holding a sheet cake in her hands. She tilted it toward him so he could see the frosting script— *Congratulations to Duke's Newest Star!*

She's just assuming it's going to happen, he thought. The scout hasn't even seen me play and already I'm enrolled. His mother tilted the cake pan back and forth, grinning.

The sight of all that chocolate sent a spike of hot bile up his throat. He hadn't gotten to puke the Pop-Tarts this morning. He couldn't with Terry in the stall with him. Christ. Not Terry, just Seth's brain fart. Anyway, they were still in his stomach, all six of them, and the idea of adding a piece of cake to the mix wasn't a pleasant one.

"Your coach called with the news!" his mother exclaimed as soon as Seth opened the car door. "Your dad came home early to celebrate!" As soon as the words left her mouth, a basketball bounced off his shoulder—his dad's favorite greeting.

"Bring the car all the way into the garage," his dad called. "I want to get in a little one-on-one tonight. We need to get you in top form for that scout."

"Great. Yeah." Yeah. All that food would feel absolutely wonderful bouncing up and down in his gut while they played. Seth got back in the car and pulled into the garage.

"You think your dad might let me play?" the Terry thing asked. "He always liked me." Seth couldn't stop himself from taking a quick glance to his right. Terry gave him a half salute.

He's wearing the same clothes, Seth realized. Not the suit from the funeral but the clothes he was wearing the day I shot him. It felt like two giant hands had taken hold of Seth's rib cage and were squeezing, squeezing, squeezing. Seth grabbed his backpack. He could feel the weight of the box of Pop-Tarts. His fingers itched to reach in and tear open the box. While he was shoving down the pastry, his world would go white and soundless and almost blank, reduced to the sensations, the pain, the fullness. He needed that, needed it now.

Seth unzipped the backpack, his breaths coming too fast. But when he saw the date written in those huge black letters he hesitated. He silently counted to ten, the way the counselor at his last school—the one his parents had no clue Seth had even spoken to—had suggested, zipped the backpack again, and got out of the car.

"Think you can take me?" his dad asked.

"Cake first," his mom said firmly.

"Actually, the coach told me I should take a bath with Epsom salts when I got home. My ankle's acting up a little." He'd figured out a long time ago that if he wanted to get out of something, it was best to play the sports injury card. Seth's ankle was almost like another member of the family—it was discussed that often, worried over that much.

"Got to do what the coach says," his father answered. "Get on in there."

"Thanks for making the cake, Mom," Seth said. "I'll eat a big piece later."

"Oh, tell the truth," Terry jumped in. "You'll hoover up the whole thing and make up a story about how the dog jumped on the counter and ate it." Seth could feel a flush creeping up the back of his neck. He had done that once, a couple years ago. But how could Terry know that?

Christ, he knows that because he's a piece of garbage from your own head, Seth told himself. What you know, he knows. Seth went inside, put his backpack in the hall closet and shut the door, then went into the bathroom. He yanked off his sweatshirt and tossed it on the floor, unbuckled his belt, then hesitated. Terry was just sitting on the toilet seat, watching.

"What?" Terry said. "I've seen you naked before. We used to take baths together."

Seth stepped right up to the toilet and crouched down so his face was only inches away from Terry's. "You are not real," he said through gritted teeth. "I do not want you here. I do not want to see you ever again. I am going to close my eyes and count to ten. When I open them, you *will* be gone."

He straightened up, shut his eyes, and began to count as slowly as he could without feeling like a complete chickenshit. When he reached ten, he opened his eyes . . . and Terry was gone. Seth turned in a circle, just to be sure. No Terry.

Of course there was no Terry. Seth turned on the hot and cold water—heavy on the hot—then stripped down. He climbed into the tub and rested his head on his mom's plastic pillow. The heat felt good, soaking into his bones. Seth closed his eyes and drifted off to sleep.

When he dreamed, he dreamed of fire.

Vicki Callison sat at her kitchen table eating an orange-spice muffin and going through the family photo albums. Each time she found a picture of Andrea, she removed it. When she'd finished with the last album, she picked up the pair of scissors sitting next to her cup of caramel mocha coffee.

Carefully, she trimmed Andrea out of the first picture. Then, snip, she cut off Andrea's head. You ruined my life, she thought. She picked up the next photo. Trim, snip, smile.

Stuffed bears. Stuffed rabbits. Stuffed monkeys. Balloon bouquets. Chocolates. Magazines. Paperbacks. Coloring books. What to get an ex-boyfriend who just came out of a coma? Tavia wondered, barely able to hold back a hysterical giggle. Keep it together, she told herself. The hospital gift shop isn't the place to have a breakdown. You'd be whisked up to the psych ward in no time.

She glanced at the clock. Five after six. She'd told Elijah's mom she'd come for a visit at six. And she couldn't get herself out of the gift shop. The place wasn't that much bigger than her bedroom, and she'd been in here for forty-five minutes, but she hadn't been able to make a decision.

"Not finding what you want?" the candy striper behind the counter asked. Tavia couldn't remember her name, but she knew the girl was Lucy Choi's little sister. On an island the size of Raven's Point, you always had a pretty good idea who everyone was. And this girl, whatever her name was, knew who Tavia was too. Tavia could see it in the girl's eyes. They were avid, eager. She wanted all the juice on Tavia and Elijah and what was going to happen now.

Tavia grabbed a roll of LifeSavers and thrust a dollar into the girl's hand. She rushed out of the gift shop without waiting for change. The sign for the ladies room caught her eye, and she stepped inside. She was late, but she needed just one more minute to get herself together before she saw Elijah.

A little splash of cold water on the face, and I'll be fine, Tavia told herself. She stuck the LifeSavers on the little metal ledge under the mirror, twisted the cold water faucet, then immediately shut the water off. She'd spent almost an hour getting her makeup right. Washing it off made no sense. Except then she could stay down here and fix it. . . .

Oh, grow a backbone, she ordered herself. Get yourself up to his room. Tavia snatched up the LifeSavers, then stared down at her hand as if she'd grabbed a scorpion. Cinnamon. She'd bought cinnamon. Tavia's fingers shook as she found the little red string and pulled it, opening the candy. The spicy smell brought a memory so powerful she had trouble staying on her feet.

"Sorry," a guy Tavia thought was Vince Pullman's cousin said. Then he stepped on her foot again. Why couldn't people just stay in their seats until the credits were over and the lights came on? Tavia thought while she gave the guy a tight, it's-okay smile.

Elijah shifted slightly in his seat, and his shoulder lost contact with hers. The stretch of skin where his body had touched hers felt cold without the heat of him. He hadn't tried to hold her hand or put his arm around her—Tavia had been all wound up waiting—but that little bit of shoulder-to-shoulder contact had set off sensations in her that she hadn't been expecting. She'd never realized a guy could touch your arm and set off a ripple that made it all the way through your body.

Tavia heard a soft whispery sound, then Elijah turned his head away from her. The lights in the movie theater came up, and Tavia saw that Elijah had a roll of cinnamon

LifeSavers in his hand. He blushed, actually blushed. "Want one?" he mumbled, holding out the candy to her.

"Um, sure," Tavia said. She stuck one of the chalky white LifeSavers into her mouth. And sitting there, next to Elijah, in the now-empty movie theater, she became hyper-conscious of her mouth—the softness of the inside of her cheeks; the tingling the cinnamon started up on her tongue; the light, light pressure where her lips met.

"I—this is stupid, but I always end up telling you every stupid thing that goes through my head," Elijah blurted out. "I bought these"—he waved the roll of LifeSavers— "because I didn't want my breath to reek if, you know, you decided you wanted to kiss me."

Tavia's stomach gave a slow roll. "If I decided? Am I deciding?"

"Well, yeah. Who else? I mean, it's a given I want to kiss you, so you're the one who . . . " Elijah's hazel eyes flicked down to Tavia's lips. Her stomach did that roll again. My first kiss, ever, she thought. It's going to happen. Most girls had had some kind of kissing experience before they got to be thirteen. Had Elijah kissed a lot of girls? Would he know that . . .

Tavia's throat went dry. She swallowed hard, and the LifeSaver got stuck in her throat. She started to choke, choke until her eyes started to water and her nose began to run. Elijah pounded her on the back, and she managed to spit the LifeSaver out.

"I'm sure you really want to kiss me now," Tavia said as she grabbed a napkin and started wiping off her face.

Elijah grabbed the napkin away. "Are you kidding?"

And he kissed her. Their teeth knocked, and it took Tavia a second to remember that she should open her mouth a little. But they were kissing. And Tavia couldn't believe she'd gone thirteen years without realizing that it was possible to feel this good.

Tavia looked at herself in the hospital bathroom mirror. Was she ever really thirteen? It felt like that first kiss had happened a million years ago. Except when it felt like it had happened yesterday. Tavia started to put the LifeSavers in her purse, but as if her hands had minds of their own, she took out the first candy of the roll and stuck it in her mouth. To her shock, she started to cry.

"Want a LifeSaver before we start?" Elijah asked. He stood on one side of the bed, wearing only his boxers and tube socks. Tavia stood on the other side.

She'd taken her shoes off, but that was it. She wanted to do this, she did. She was fifteen. Sixteen in a few months. She was ready. And with Elijah's parents and little sister away it was the perfect time. They'd been planning this for weeks . . .

"Tavie? LifeSaver?" Elijah repeated. She tried to answer, but she couldn't make her mouth move. "We don't have to do this now," Elijah said.

"Sure, okay, yeah, give me one." Tavia managed to hold out her hand. Elijah's fingers brushed the skin of her palm when he handed her one of the candies, and Tavia felt her stomach do that flip, and she knew that this was really what she wanted.

"Oh, and I almost forgot. Mood music." Elijah fumbled in the drawer of his nightstand and pulled out a CD. He

*stuck it in his boom box, and a second later *NSYNC
began to play.*

*Tavia laughed. Laughed until her eyes started to water
and her nose began to run. Elijah was the only one who
knew the dirty secret of her love of *NSYNC. He knew all
the little things about her that were so not Tavia Burrows.
Except he thought that they were exactly Tavia. He loved
discovering some goofy thing about her.*

*"Shut that off," Tavia finally managed to say, wiping
her face with both hands. "I'm not going to be remember-
ing 'Bye Bye Bye' playing when I think about my first
time."*

*Elijah pulled the plug on the boom box. He grabbed a
condom off his nightstand, scrambled over the bed, and
stood up next to Tavia. His face got serious for a moment,
then he smiled. "I think if we're going to do this, you have
to take off more than your shoes. Not that I have much, or
any, actual experience here, but I'm pretty sure that—"*

*"You definitely have to take off those ratty tube socks,"
Tavia interrupted.*

The bathroom door swung open, pulling Tavia away
from her memories. What an awkward, messy, somewhat
painful, somewhat amazing night that had been.

Six months later, Elijah was in a coma.

Tavia took another look at herself in the mirror. It was
clear she'd been crying. She did what she could with makeup, then left the bathroom, strode over to the elevator, and
pushed the Up button twice. She'd wasted enough time. She
was late. It was time to see Elijah.

We might not have even still been together at this point,

she told herself as she waited for the elevator. And even if we were, this would be the last of it. We'd both be going off to college. No little high school romance survives four years of college, probably colleges in separate states.

The elevator doors slid open. Tavia stepped on and punched the button for the seventh floor. Elijah will understand that, she thought. And he'll understand that it's been more than a year and a half. He won't expect me to—

The elevator reached the seventh floor. Weird that Raven's Point even had a hospital with seven floors. Some Englishman who'd emigrated to the island, a second son with no title but a lot of money, had built the hospital back in the day, and had left enough money to keep the place up-to-date. Once in a while a celeb looking for extreme privacy came to the hospital to detox from whatever his substance of choice was, and occasionally one of the summer tourists broke a bone or something, but mostly only island people used the hospital. Which meant it was mostly empty.

Tavia straightened her spine, squared her shoulders, and turned down the left-hand corridor. The first person she saw was Elijah's dad. And it was clear from his expression that he did expect her to have waited, to have been the loyal girlfriend, to have grown into a crone by Elijah's bedside and died there if that's how long he'd stayed unconscious.

Elijah's sister, Jane, jumped up from her plastic chair. "Tavia, hi," she exclaimed. "Mom's in with Elijah, but I'll go get her out."

Before Tavia had time to say that she didn't mind waiting, really, not at all, Jane had disappeared into

Elijah's hospital room.

"Hello, Mr. Romano," Tavia said, because she'd seen him, and he'd seen her see him, so she had to say something.

"Nice to see you again," he answered.

Was she being paranoid, or was there a little too much emphasis on *again*? As in it's been months since you visited my son, whom you claimed to love.

"Tavia, sweetie." Mrs. Romano hurried out of Elijah's room and gave her a quick, tight hug. "Go on in. Elijah's getting a little tired, but he's excited that you're here."

Tavia nodded, unable to come up with any more words. If it was this strange and strained talking to Elijah's parents, how was she going to make it through talking to Elijah himself? She walked directly into his room, passing Jane on Jane's way out, then sat down in the plastic chair next to Elijah's bed, the same chair she'd sat in every day for six months and eleven days. Until she couldn't take it anymore. Until she had to break away or die herself.

Look at him, she ordered herself. You owe him that. Tavia raised her eyes and met Elijah's, and for the first time in so long she could feel him looking back at her.

"Hi." It took almost all her strength to get that one word out. But suddenly more words tumbled free, as if a dam at the back of her throat had broken. "I've been going out with Thomas Bledsoe. Remember him? School paper. Marching band. Only for a few weeks. But I have . . . been going out with him."

"Whoa." Elijah shoved his sandy brown hair off his forehead. "Okay. Well, at least you didn't ask how I'm feeling. I've already answered that about a thousand times."

31

Tavia twisted her hands together in her lap, squeezing so hard the small bones of her fingers began to ache. "I'm sorry. I don't know why I blurted that out. I didn't mean to just . . . I'm sorry." She pulled in a long breath, trying to compose herself. "You look great." And he actually did. She'd expected his body to have become more wasted, his face even thinner. But it was like he'd gotten some super-strength extreme-health infusion.

"You look different," Elijah said.

"It's the hair. Longer. Braids," Tavia answered.

"No. Well, yeah, but that's not it." He studied her until Tavia wanted to squirm in her seat. "I don't know. There's something."

"And you. I thought you'd be really out of it. I didn't think you could just come out of a coma and seem so normal." Tavia forced her hands apart.

"I'm a medical wonder," Elijah told her. "You wouldn't believe how many doctors have been through here. A few have already taken the ferry over from Rhode Island. Some specialist is flying in from New York tomorrow. I guess I shouldn't be in such good shape, more muscle atrophy for starters."

"That's great. That's wonderful." Should I touch him? Tavia thought. Was I supposed to hug him when I came in? Am I still, now that I told him about Thomas? She poured herself a glass of water, just so she'd have something to do while she was trying to figure out what was right. "Want some water, Elijah? Or I could get you something else."

Elijah didn't answer. He'd turned his face toward the window.

Tavia waited. And waited. The only sound was her own heartbeat pounding in her ears. "Elijah?" she finally whispered. Could he have fallen asleep so quickly. Or, oh god, could he be crying, or just so hurt that he didn't want her to see his face? He hadn't seemed that upset, but—

"Elijah?" Tavia said, a little more loudly. No answer. She pushed herself to her feet and walked around to the other side of the bed. Elijah stared straight ahead, his hazel eyes blank. Tavia reached out and gave his shoulder a little shake, suddenly terrified he'd sunk back into whatever dark place he'd been all these months.

"I think you'd better go," Elijah said flatly.

"No, please, Elijah. Let me stay. Let me just sit here if you don't want to talk," Tavia begged. "I shouldn't have sprung it on you about Thomas. You know I care—"

"I think you'd better go." Elijah closed his eyes. "I'm tired."

Tavia stared at him for a moment, hoping he'd open his eyes and really look at her again. But he didn't. So Tavia picked up her purse and left the room. "He was too tired to visit anymore," she called in the direction of Elijah's family and kept on walking. She took the stairs down to the lobby, not wanting to wait for the elevator.

"Tavia, over here. I just wanted to make sure you were okay." Thomas got up from one of the long padded benches near the electric doors. He wrapped his arms around her and pulled her close. "How're you doing, Eight?"

Eight. He called her eight because her full name was Octavia and he wanted to have a special nickname that no one—meaning Elijah—had ever called her.

"Fine, I think," Tavia answered. Thomas was the last person she wanted to talk to about Elijah. She waited a few seconds, then gently pulled away.

"Do you want to maybe get something to eat? The clam shack? I know how you love that even the Cokes taste like fish there."

Sweet. He's really sweet, Tavia thought. But she couldn't take sweet right now. If she had to be around sweet for two more minutes she'd start to blubber again. "I'm really tired," she told him. "I just want to go home and sleep."

"It's still early—" Thomas began, then he stopped himself. "I'll walk you to your car."

Thomas didn't try to kiss her before she got into the rusted-out Toyota, and she was grateful. She rolled the window partway down as she pulled out of her parking space. "See you at school," she called.

She was halfway home before she realized she was driving with the headlights off. She flicked them on just in time to see a cat streaking across the street.

The weirdness of her morning run rushed back to her. She hadn't thought about it all day. The second she'd arrived at school, Mrs. Moya, the principal, had pulled her aside and told her about Elijah. And pretty much the only thought she'd had from then on was of her boyfriend. Former boyfriend.

Did Elijah remember me breaking up with him? Tavia wondered. Could he hear me reading off my list of reasons as I sat next to his bed and held his hand?

She couldn't think about that now. Her head would just

split open if she tried. Tavia pulled into her driveway. So that weirdness with the animals, she thought, trying to distract herself, wonder what was with that. If I was in some sci-fi movie, it would turn out that they were obeying me because I was actually half alien or something.

Tavia paused by the little koi pond under the willow tree in the front yard and spread her arms out wide. "Jump fish," she commanded. "Come to me, your extraterrestrial mistress."

A small bubble appeared near the center of the pond. Then popped. Two more formed. Then popped. Five more. Pop, pop, pop, pop, pop. It was like the whole pond was resting on a hot stove. The water looked as if it were boiling.

It's because of the fish, Tavia realized. All the fish had darted to the surface. One, shiny gold in the moonlight, leapt onto the grass, then thrashed there, suffocating.

Tavia scooped it up, almost dropping the slithering thing, and tossed it back into the pool. But six more fish had already landed at her feet. Another arched through the air and landed on her shoe. All their little fish mouths were open in round circles as they gasped for oxygen.

"No!" Tavia cried. She fell to her knees and began pushing the fish back into the pond. "Stay in the water. Stay in the water!"

When the last orange fish was back in the pond, Tavia still sat on the ground. That didn't just happen, she told herself. Although she could see the indentations in the grass where the fish had helplessly flopped around, round mouths opening and closing. "That did *not* just happen."

She said it aloud this time, hoping that it would somehow convince her.

It didn't. But she pretended that it had. She stood up, brushed the dirt off her corduroy pants, and headed into the house.

Her mother gave her about two seconds before she started with the questions. "How was it seeing Elijah? How is he?"

"He's doing great," Tavia answered. "Miracle cure, it seems. Doctors flying in to study him and everything. Probably extra ferry runs to bring over all the reporters." She forced a smile, one of the many smiles she'd pushed her lips into that day. "We'll talk in the morning, okay? I have to study."

When she was finally alone in her room, Tavia let out a breath she hadn't even realized she'd been holding. She shut off the lights, lay down on her bed fully clothed, and pulled the half of the comforter she wasn't lying on over her. Then she focused all her attention on the sound of the ocean. The rhythmic crash of the waves in the distance always lulled her to sleep. All she wanted was to sleep. But it took hours for sleep to come.

When it did, she dreamed of fire.

Billy Whitcomb headed down to the kitchen. The bait traps needed to be refilled and this was the best time to do it, because the kitchen workers were on their break. Billy knew everything about the hospital. That's why when something needed to be done, you called on Billy the handyman. The handy man. He liked that. He liked being handy.

Useful. He liked going home at the end of the day feeling like he'd done something.

"Handy Billy, the handyman," he sang to himself as he took the box of poison out of the highest cupboard. There were ten bait trays in the kitchen, and he knew where each one was. He pulled the first out from under the stove and started to shake out some fresh blue pellets. Then he paused.

Was this really the best way to kill roaches? Roaches had no place in a hospital. And wouldn't he be more sure that the roaches were really and truly dead if he killed them by hand?

Billy sat down on the floor and waited. It didn't take long. A roach skittered out from under the sink. Billy snatched it up. Crunch, squish, dead. Usually just looking at roaches, with their shiny brown bodies and their little thread legs, gave him the wiggins. But now he realized it was kind of fun to take care of them by hand.

He waited patiently for the next roach to show its little roach face. Crunch, squish, smile.

"You're really talking about me," Jane's mother said.

Jane's dad put down the copy of *Newsweek* he'd just picked up.

Jane's teeth squeaked as she ground them together. Whenever people argued she always started with the teeth grinding. It didn't even matter if she didn't know them. She could be in a movie, sitting in front of two total strangers—as much as people could be total strangers in Raven's Point—and they'd start bickering about something stupid, like whether or not it was okay to talk during the coming attractions, and squeak, squeak, squeak, Jane's teeth would be rubbing together.

"All I said was it was surprising that Tavia completely stopped visiting Elijah," Jane's dad said. "Even if she wanted to start going out with someone else, you think she'd keep visiting once in a while, just as a friend."

"I know that's what you said," Jane's mother answered. "But we both know what you meant was that I haven't been visiting Elijah enough. Not the way you, his sainted father, have."

"You visit a lot, Mom," Jane jumped in. "And you made that quilt for his bed, with his favorite colors and everything."

Jane's father ducked behind the *Newsweek*. Jane's mother looked like she wasn't finished arguing yet. "I'm just going to run to the gift shop for some gum," Jane announced. A layer of gum between her upper and lower teeth would help. She gave her dad a squeeze on the arm as she passed him, an I-know-you've-totally-been-there-for-Elijah squeeze.

She walked the seven flights down to the lobby—she was in no hurry. She stopped to take a drink at the fountain, then meandered down the empty hall. Wonder if Dad's finished his magazine yet, she thought, idly running her finger over the brass plaque that read RAVEN'S POINT HOSPITAL. FOUNDED 1892. I should get him another one to keep him occu—

Jane blinked. Then blinked again. "What is . . . " She couldn't complete the thought. She needed to sit down. But the padded benches that usually flanked this hallway were gone. And the hallway wasn't a hallway anymore.

She was standing in a ward, she guessed you'd call it, with a double row of beds. Gaslight lit the room. And the smell—it wasn't the smell of antiseptic with a little food and urine and sickness mixed in. No, with every breath, Jane was taking in the odor of rotting meat. It was like the time they'd gone on vacation for two weeks and come back to a broken fridge and a pile of roast, chicken, and steaks that were on the slimy road to decomposition.

A short woman in a floor-length skirt and a long-sleeved blouse hurried past Jane carrying a glass bowl. Jane's mind raced, trying to come up with an explanation for what she was seeing.

"Who are you?" she called after the woman. "Is this some kind of history exhibit, like at Colonial Williamsburg?" Jane had gone to Colonial Williamsburg with her scout troop when she was ten. They'd made butter with a churn and everything. This could be something like that—

Except the smell. A hospital wouldn't allow that smell. Another woman, taller than the first, brushed past Jane without acknowledging her. She joined the first woman at the second bed in the first row.

The taller woman tied a piece of cloth around the arm of the man who lay in the bed. Then she removed a thin knife from her pocket. Calmly she cut a slit several inches long in the man's arm. He howled with pain.

"What are you doing to him?" Jane cried. Neither woman answered or looked her way. The shorter of the women positioned the glass bowl so it would catch the man's blood and tenderly laid her other hand on his forehead as his blood gushed from his body.

Jane closed her eyes and scrubbed her face with her fingers. When she lowered her hands and opened her eyes, she found herself in the hallway again, standing next to the plaque, the one that said RAVEN'S POINT HOSPITAL. FOUNDED 1892.

Eighteen ninety-two. They would have used gaslight in 1892. And the clothes seemed right for that year, from what Jane could remember of the pictures in her history book.

Wait. Stop, Jane told herself. You can't be standing here trying to decide if you could have gone back in time more than a hundred years. That's insane. Literally. And that's exactly what your parents need—their daughter being committed on the day their son finally comes out of a coma.

Jane returned to the drinking fountain and sucked down water until her mouth felt numb. Then she returned to her parents. "Elijah's still asleep," her mother told her. "Maybe you should go home and get some rest. We could call you a taxi."

"That's okay," Jane said quickly. There was no way she was sleeping in the house by herself. Not when she'd recently had a psychotic episode. Make that two, she corrected herself. It was only this morning that she'd thought she was back in the Caddy during the accident. It felt like a million years ago, but it was only this morning.

"Well, at least try to take a little nap yourself," her mother answered.

Jane nodded. She sat down in the empty chair between

her mother and father. Even though she thought there was zero chance of falling asleep, she leaned her head back against the wall and closed her eyes. Sleep came almost instantly.

When it came, she dreamed of fire.

Chapter 3

Normal Isn't Normal

"Do you agree that tragedy has to involve a fall from a great height, such as the king's in *Lear*? Or do you think an ordinary man, with a shorter distance to fall—such as Willy Loman in *Death of a Salesman*—can be a truly tragic figure?" Mr. Hennessy asked in his monotone. "That is your essay question. Essay due in two weeks."

Seth dutifully copied the question into his notebook, then glanced at the clock. Only two minutes left of his AP English class. How did that happen? Usually this class crawled by. Maybe it was just because after yesterday's madness, normal felt great. Sitting here, trying to stay awake through an hour of Hennessy's droning was a slam dunk.

The minute hand on the clock clicked and everybody started gathering their stuff together in anticipation of the bell. Hennessy kept on talking, but class was clearly over.

Seth jammed his notebook in his backpack, catching a glimpse of the Pop-Tart box. He felt absolutely no desire to crack it open. He'd have that box sitting on his dresser in the old folks' home. They could stick it in his coffin with him.

The bell rang, and Seth slid out of the desk that was too low for someone his height. His legs always ended up falling asleep. But today even the pins and needles shooting through him felt good. Normal. He was likin' normal.

"Seth," a girl called just as he made it out the classroom door. Seth turned his head and saw Andrea Callison smiling at him. She hurried over. "Can you give me that essay question?" she asked. "I kind of spaced during class. Hennessy's voice puts me in a trance or something, and I only wrote part of it down."

"Uh, sure." Seth knew that Andrea had a bunch of girl-friends in the class who could give her the info. In fact, a couple of them were hanging out farther down the hallway, shooting little looks at him and Andrea. But there was nothing to do but dig out his notebook and flip it open to the question.

Andrea stepped a little closer to him. "I'll just copy it down really quick."

Seth didn't answer. He stood there breathing through his mouth so he'd get a little less of her perfume. It was so flowery it made him want to sneeze.

"Um, excuse me. I just need to get in . . . " That girl, the one with the fluffy light brown hair who he always saw at games, nodded toward the locker he and Andrea were blocking.

"Sure." Seth backed up a few steps. Andrea followed him, using the move to stand even closer.

Seth's eyes flicked to the fluffy-haired girl. Jane, that was her name. All he really knew about her was that she was the one with the brother in the coma and that her brother used to be on the team. But there was something about her . . . The way she stood back and watched everything. It always made him wonder what she was thinking.

"Thanks," Andrea said when she'd finished writing. "Oh, and congratulations on getting scouted. That's great!" She gave his arm a little squeeze, and Seth felt his chest tighten. Being around her, being around most girls at school, made him want to bolt.

He shot another glance at Jane, and his body loosened up a little. She wasn't like other girls. Maybe because she'd had to deal with more than most girls had. Sometimes if he was stressing on the court, he'd make sure and look for her at halftime. Just finding her in the stands . . . it did something to him. She'd kind of turned into a lucky charm, even though he'd never talked to her.

"So, to the cafeteria?" Andrea asked, acting as if they ate together all the time. Seth knew the girl wanted to hook up with him. The guys on the team were always mocking him for not getting in her pants, when she practically unzipped them for him.

"I'm gonna—I need to run an errand," Seth told her. He was such a loser. Andrea had all that red hair, and her skin was unbelievably smooth—definitely something he'd like to get his hands on. And her breasts—looking at her face when she talked to him was a challenge.

"Want company?" Andrea asked.

Say yes, Seth thought. Why not? She's falling all over herself to be with you.

But she didn't know him. All she knew was that he was on the basketball team. And that she liked the way he looked or whatever. She didn't know what he'd done. The tightness in his chest increased. He had to get out of here. "No. It'd be too boring for you," Seth told Andrea. "Thanks though."

He turned away from the cafeteria and headed for the main exit, passing a couple of freshmen guys on the way. They looked at him like . . . basically like they wanted to climb into his skin and be him, for chrissake. His chest now felt three times smaller than the rest of his body, too small to hold his heart and lungs. His heart felt like it was struggling to beat, and he could pull only a little air into his flattened lungs with every breath.

He shifted his backpack on his shoulder, and he could feel the box in there. His feet pivoted, and Seth was walking into the closest bathroom. He hadn't decided to go there. His body had. The bathroom wasn't empty, but there was a stall free. Seth's feet took him inside. His hands locked the door and pulled out the box of Pop-Tarts. His breathing came a little easier just holding it.

Okay, count to ten, Seth told himself. You can eat them all and the friggin' box. Just count to ten first. Sometimes this actually worked for him. Not always, but once in a while. He began to count, mouthing the numbers. When he reached ten, he managed to take control of his own body again. He returned the Pop-Tarts to his backpack.

It was almost a rerun of yesterday, he realized. But he'd triumphed over the tarts. And he hadn't brain-farted out a ghost. Things were looking up. But Seth didn't feel quite ready to leave the bathroom. The stall, yes. The bathroom, no.

It was empty now. Safe. Seth turned on the cold water, noting that some genius had clogged the sink with paper towels. He cupped his hands under the stream, then splashed his face with the water. The cold felt good on his skin. And his chest was almost back to its usual size, his heart and lungs getting some room.

He stuck his hands under the water again. It was crimson. It was blood.

Seth jerked his head up and stared at himself in the mirror. Streaks of the blood were running down his face. He could taste salt on his lips. He could taste the blood. Saliva flooded his mouth, and he knew he was about to puke.

"Can't be happening. Can't be happening," he muttered. He swallowed hard, trying to get a grip on himself, then twisted the cold water tap shut. The blood stopped flowing. But it had filled the clogged sink, thick and smelling of copper.

All Seth wanted to do was get out of there, but he couldn't stop staring at the blood, compelled, fascinated. The blood began to swirl. It's going to go down the drain, Seth thought. Then it'll be over.

But the swirls didn't form the usual whirlpool. They formed a mouth, and the mouth began to scream. The sound—low and grief filled—broke the strange hold on Seth. He bolted.

Terry Reingold stood blocking the door. "Are you sure you wouldn't rather talk to me? The others aren't all so friendly."

"Get the hell away from me!" Seth shouted.

"Okay, okay. Have it your way." Terry disappeared.

Seth stepped into the hall, and got a couple looks, that were like "what was the shouting about?" But no one was reacting to the blood. Seth checked his hands. Clean. He felt his face. Clean.

Is this what insanity feels like from the inside? he wondered.

Then he saw her, his lucky girl. Jane. Just walking down the hall. And it was like an ocean breeze had started up. Cooling him off. Making him feel clean. Without thinking, he followed her.

Handy Billy, the handyman, sat in the hospital basement next to the boiler. He held a piece of cheese in one outstretched hand. Come on, little ratty, Billy thought. Come on over. Billy's your friend.

The rat eyed the cheese. Eyed Billy. Billy could tell it was about ready to come to him. Billy had been statue still for at least an hour, maybe more.

One little paw moved forward. Another little paw moved forward. Yes, yes, yes, Billy thought. Just a little closer, ratty boy.

Billy's fingers began to tremble with eagerness. But he waited. Waited.

Then grabbed. Twisted. Heard the little squeal. Heard

the little neck bone crack. It was much better to deal with these things by hand.

"Tell us about the accident?" "What was the first thing your brother said when he came to?" "Did you think Elijah would ever come out of the coma?" "Would you call it a miracle?"

Camera flashes went off, half blinding Jane. Where had all these reporters come from? They couldn't all be from the Raven's Point paper.

"Jane, one of the nurses told me your father visited Elijah every single day since the accident. Is that true?" a reporter asked. Jane realized that this reporter was flanked by a guy with a camera on his shoulder.

"You should talk to my parents," Jane called out, "or Elijah's doctor. They can tell you more." God, it was like they wanted her to rip open her chest and hand them her still-beating heart. She didn't know if her parents would want any kind of story written at all.

"Just one question. Did you ever—"

"Jane, come on. We're late." And a hand grabbed Jane's arm. She looked up and saw Seth McFadden, senior god. How could someone like him even know her name?

"Come on," Seth repeated. He gave her arm a gentle tug and they were running down the school's wide front steps, weaving through the reporters, then flying across the grass and over to the parking lot. Seth unlocked the passenger door of a green car—Jane didn't know what kind. "Get in," he told her. So she did.

And they were out of there.

During the great escape, Jane had almost forgotten for a second who she was with. Now it all came rushing back. She was in a car. Not three feet from—Seth McFadden. "Thanks," she offered up. It was lame, but it was better than just staring at him.

"Hungry?" Seth asked. "I'm thinking the drive-through."

"Sure." Like she was going to say no. She wasn't crazy. Or, well, maybe she was. Maybe this was just a funnier episode of her delusions. If it were, she'd worry about it later.

She was relieved when Seth turned on the radio. It meant she had to do some head bobbing that felt kind of retarded, but she didn't have to talk, and that was good, because what did she have to say to a guy like Seth McFadden? Just today she'd seen him cozied up in the hallway with Andrea Callison, the most beautiful girl in . . . in ever.

Does he know I go to every Ravens' basketball game just to see him? Jane couldn't help thinking. Please don't let him, she prayed. That would be so humiliating.

I'm sure he never noticed you, she told herself, trying to calm down. Or if he did, maybe he thought you just went to the games because Elijah used to be on the team.

"How about if we just eat in the car?" Seth asked as he pulled into the line at the drive-through window.

"Sure," Jane answered. How many times had she said "sure" in the last ten minutes? Would he think she didn't know any other words? Is that why he wanted to eat in the car? Was she too embarrassing to be seen with? There were always a bunch of the older kids eating lunch in there.

"What are you having?" Seth said. And Jane had the feeling he'd already asked her once. Pay attention, she told herself. At least try to give the appearance of normalcy.

"Burger. Onion rings. Chocolate shake," she told him, blurting out her usual order without censoring. God, would he think she was a total pig? Onion rings and a shake. What was she thinking?

"'Serving happy customers since nineteen fifty-two,'" Seth said, reading off the side of the building. "Do you think they're still using the same french fry grease or do you think they change it every decade?"

A girl in tight pants and a short red jacket with gold buttons glided by on roller skates and hooked a metal tray to the window of the car in front of Jane. She wore a hat that looked like a big hamburger. The girl definitely wasn't from the twenty-first century.

Not now. Not here, please, Jane thought. Then Seth shook a bag of food in front of her face. They were past the window and parked in the lot. And it was definitely 2004 again.

What happens to me when I do that? Does my face go all slack and stupid? She shot a glance at Seth, but he was calmly putting mustard on his burger, not acting as if he'd let a loon into his car.

Seth cleared his throat. He hesitated, like he was trying to come up with something to say. But that couldn't be it. A guy like Seth wouldn't worry about talking. He'd just *talk*. "Some guys on the team are going to visit your brother tonight," he said. "I wasn't sure if I should go, since I started school after, you know, the accident."

"Don't worry about that," Jane told him. "Elijah won't care." But wait, did that sound like she was pressuring him? "It's okay if you don't go too," she added. "Like you said, you don't know him or anything."

Jane picked up her burger. She wished she'd ordered something else. The burgers here were really thick, which meant you had to open your mouth really wide, and how attractive could that be? She lowered the burger. "So, what do you think of Raven's Point? Are you glad you moved here?"

Seth hesitated again. "It's small. I like that," he finally said.

"Really? You wouldn't rather go to a bigger school, be on a better team?" Jane went for one of her onion rings.

"Nah." Seth took a bite of his burger. A piece of may-onnaisey lettuce fell onto his lap. "These things are massive. Don't they know that no one has the jaw capacity to handle them?"

Who would have thunk it? Jane felt a small smile tug-ging at her mouth. Seth McFadden, senior god, and I have something in common. Only our hatred of the thickness of the burgers here, but it's something.

Should I put him out of his misery? Tavia wondered. Should I just give him every detail of my visit with Elijah? It wasn't like anything had happened that Thomas couldn't hear. In fact, he would be relieved to know that Tavia had already told Elijah that the two of them were going out.

Tavia took a bite of her tuna sandwich, stalling. She

didn't think she could do it. She didn't think she could even say the name Elijah in front of Thomas.

"I need to study for my French quiz," Thomas said. "Come to the library with me?"

That's how it had started. She and Thomas. Just studying together. Nothing more. Back when Tavia was still the grieving near-widow, back when everyone automatically stopped laughing and started talking more softly whenever they saw her.

Tavia held up her sandwich. "I'm not finished yet."

"Sorry. Duh. I'll wait," Thomas said.

"No, go ahead. I'll meet up with you," Tavia told him. She could use a break from his sweet puppy dog eyes, always looking at her, always wanting something from her.

Thomas is a great guy, she reminded herself as he gave her a little kiss on the cheek. "See you there." Thomas swung his backpack onto his shoulder. "Hey, do you have gum or a mint or anything? I've got pepperoni breath."

Tavia reached into her purse and felt around. Her fingers brushed against the roll of cinnamon LifeSavers she'd bought at the hospital, and her stomach did a slow flip. "Sorry. All out," she told Thomas. "But here." She grabbed a piece of parsley off her plate. "Eat this. It's a natural breath freshener."

"Sweet." Thomas popped the parsley in his mouth and headed out of the caf. It took less than a minute for Andrea Callison to take his seat, her entourage—Madeline Gunderson, Lucy Choi, and Elizabeth Reynolds—gathering around her.

"How was it seeing Elijah?" Madeline burst out. "Was

it weird? Did he look weird?"

"God, Madeline." Lucy flashed Tavia an apologetic smile. "What my socially damaged friend here meant to say was, how are you?"

You want all the dirt too, Tavia thought. Madeline's just more honest about it. "He was really tired. But feeling good, amazingly good."

"What did you guys talk about?" Andrea asked. "Did he want to know how the basketball team's been doing? Or, like, current-events kinds of things?"

"Or did he want to know what you've been doing with yourself?" Lucy added.

Tavia really didn't want to talk to Andrea and company. They weren't her friends. But maybe if she gave them a few crumbs, they'd go away. Except what crumb could she give them—the fact that she'd immediately announced that she was going out with another guy? "Like I said, he was really tired. I only saw him for a few minutes."

Andrea leaned forward. "Tavia, we just wanted to say that you don't have to worry about any of us saying anything to Elijah. We'll make sure the guys don't say anything either."

"What?" Tavia shook her head.

"We won't say anything about you and Thomas," Madeline answered. "It's not like you two were together very long or anything."

So, I'm just supposed to break up with him, that's what they think, Tavia realized. Which really wouldn't be so hard to do. And then she was supposed to run back to Elijah. That wasn't her, though. She wasn't the kind of girl who found the love of her life in high school. She was off to college in less than a year. She had plans. Plans that didn't involve a guy of any kind.

"Wait a second," Elizabeth said. "You *are* breaking up with Thomas, aren't you?"

Andrea, Lucy, Madeline, and Elizabeth stared at her, waiting, wanting Tavia to tell all, to just open herself up and let them poke around in her heart.

I can't, Tavia thought. I won't be able to keep control of myself.

Birds. The thought surprised her, but she went with it. *Birds come closer*, she silently ordered, trying to shove the command out of her brain and into the air.

She didn't really expect anything to happen. But she wasn't completely surprised when the flapping of hundreds of wings drowned out the conversation in the cafeteria, the warm powdery smell of the birds filtering into the room, blending with the odors of pizza, tuna, peanut butter, burgers, and fries.

"What are they doing?" Madeline shouted.

Stay, birds. Stay with me, Tavia silently coaxed.

The birds settled down. On the trees in the quad. On the telephone wires. On the roofs of the other buildings. On the grounds.

The eyes of everyone in the cafeteria stayed on the birds, waiting to see what they would do.

Vicki Callison dropped Andrea's head into the garbage disposal, turned on the water, flipped the switch, and ground the head up. Then she flipped off the switch, turned off the water, and reached for the pile of heads she'd trimmed from the family albums. She was disappointed to see that there was only one head left.

Savoring the moment, Vicki took the head and pressed it into the black rubber mouth of the disposal. She turned on the water, flipped the switch, and let the disposal grind. The low sound set up a delicious hum in her body.

"All gone," Vicki said in a singsong. She switched off the disposal and turned off the water. In the silence, she heard the kitchen door open. She spun around—and saw Andrea step inside.

"Not all gone," she whispered. Had she missed a head? Vicki checked the table and the counter and the floor. No, all the heads were gone. So why was Andrea still here?

She's stubborn, Vicki thought. But I'll find a way to get rid of her.

I have emerged into the sunlight. Still helpless. Defenseless. I can only wriggle on my belly. No one who sees me now could begin to imagine the power I once had. The power I will have again.

I stretch. Contract. Impatient for
my strength to grow.

Was my existence something like this when I first came to be, before I had any awareness of myself?
I have wondered about my origins, of course.
What else is there to occupy me here in the dark?

I imagine I could have been created anywhere, anywhere humans could be found, because with humans come lust and envy and hatred, the host of dark, tasty emotions I need to survive. Would I have formed in a desert? I suppose so. Eventually. But I imagine it happened faster on an island, with the humans so close together, trapped together, all that emotion building, brewing, ready to explode.

I suspect something special happened on my island. Something especially strong and juicy. All that energy couldn't go unused. That is not the way nature works. And so I came to be. For I am natural. As natural as my prey.

My prey. I cannot wait to be close to them again.
To taste.

For now, I stretch. Contract.

Then I am lifted up. And I am soaring into the air.
Climbing toward the sun. Exhilaration fills me.

Until I am dropped in a wet maw. Death so close.

I will not let this be the end. I thrust my power,
my fire, out, out, out. And I am in a new body.
Still weak. But so much stronger. Never again will
I have to crawl on my belly. And I can see now. I
can feel my heart pumping inside me.
I have bones again.

Presently, I will be stronger still. I must be patient.
It will not happen quickly.

But my time will come again.

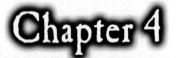

Chapter 4

Mad Cow Disease?

"**So my dad has** decided that he has to take charge of all the family TV viewing," Chad told Seth as they suited up for practice the next day after school. "He wants to control the Internet too. He actually bought that CYBERsitter software."

"Sucks," Seth answered, just saying enough to keep Chad going. He could listen to Chad rant all day. It helped him stay calm.

"My sister, the little kiss ass, pretends like it's all fine with her," Chad continued as he double-knotted his Nikes. "You ready?"

"Yep." Seth led the way out of the locker room into the gym. Most of the rest of the guys were already hanging out in the middle of the court.

"Your groupie's here," Chad teased, jerking his chin toward Andrea and her friends in the bleachers. "Are you ever gonna make a move or what?"

Seth felt a twinge in his chest, like the giant hand had just given him a little is-it-ripe test squeeze. "She's here for you," he told Chad. "It's that goatee—she's never seen one with so few hairs before. It makes her hot."

"I knew it was only a matter of time." Chad grinned and gave Andrea a slow wink. "Yeah, I can see by the way she had to work so hard to pretend she hasn't seen me that she is drawn to me like metal to a magnet."

Seth laughed. If he could keep Chad around twenty-four/seven he'd have his little insanity problem solved. It was impossible to imagine seeing a ghost or whatever with Chad in the vicinity.

Jane was like that too. He hadn't been sure how it would feel to actually talk to her—instead of shooting looks at her from the court. But she was even better up close. Eating lunch with her the other day, he'd felt like he'd entered a no-madness zone. She didn't talk a lot, not like Chad. But she had some kind of mojo working. When he was with her, he felt . . . normal.

A piercing whistle rang out, echoing through the nearly empty gym. "Okay, guys," Coach Austin yelled. "Scrimmage game today. Man-on-man defense instead of zones. Plett, stay on McFadden like he's your girlfriend. We got less than two weeks before the scout shows up, and it's going to be a group effort getting Seth ready."

"Yeah, we've all gotta be there for our Seth," Matthew said loudly, giving the coach a crap-eating grin.

The giant hand gave Seth's chest a quick, nasty crunch. Did the coach have to make practice all about him?

"Guess the coach doesn't know Plett's never had a girl-friend," Chad said under his breath. Seth choked out a laugh.

"Usual teams. Let's go, let's go," Coach Austin called.

The tallest kid in school, Ryan Ahmanson, moved to the center of the court. The third tallest kid in school, Joseph Friesly—the second tallest, Scott Marshall, was captain of the debate team and refused to even try out for basketball—took his position across from Ryan. The coach's whistle blew. The ball went up. Joseph, the center for Seth's team, won the tip-off, and an instant later, both teams were pounding down the court.

Seth's eyes never stopped moving. He liked playing point, the way you always had to be thinking, strategiz-ing—who should the ball go to now? And now? Joseph shot him the ball. Seth pivoted and passed it to Vince. "Wuss," Matthew muttered.

"Just doin' my job," Seth answered. He was supposed to see the big picture, keep the ball moving toward their basket. Vince drove the ball down the court, passed to Joseph, who was in position in front of the hoop. Joseph leapt up, threw. The ball ricocheted off the rim. Seth and Matthew launched themselves in the air, reaching for the ball.

Matthew's elbow caught Seth on the shoulder on the way down—those kind of "accidents" were a Plett specialty. And when they landed back on the floor, Matthew man-aged to come down on Seth's weak ankle. The pain shot up his body, all the way to his molars. He ignored it, pounding down the court toward the opposite basket, gluing himself to Matthew. That a-hole wasn't going to get close to the ball. Not after that little stunt. Seth could see Drew DiFrancisco trying to figure out who was open. Drew feinted left, but Seth knew the ball was gonna be coming toward Matthew.

Seth put on some speed, edging in front of Matthew, angling his shoulder so it blocked half Matthew's body. He shot a glance at Drew—

Naked. Bloody. Not Drew. An old man. Long hair and beard dripping blood onto the shiny wooden floor.

What the— How did he get out on—

The old man wobbled. Seth reached for him. But before Seth made contact, the man collapsed. He splashed when he hit the floor, his body now only a puddle of blood.

Christ. How— A man— Seth couldn't complete a thought.

"McFadden, don't just stand there with your thumb up your butt," Coach Austin hollered. "Move, move, move!"

Seth felt as if his entire body had turned to liquid, like the old man's . . . the old man who wasn't there. Seth forced himself to run on his liquid legs. Too slow. Matthew made the basket. But . . . someone on Seth's team . . . he couldn't come up with the name. His brain was liquid too. He could feel it sloshing. But the guy from his team was running toward their basket, so Seth ran with the others, running past the pool of blood that wasn't there anymore. Wha— Wh— He turned himself over to instinct and kept running. And was under the hoop again. Jumping for the ball. Getting too close to Matthew on the way down, slamming shoulders with him.

"Don't you ever touch me!" Matthew shouted.

Seth's sloshy brain tried to send out a warning, but it wasn't fast enough. Matthew slammed his fist into Seth's jaw. Shock waves swept through his face and down his neck. It almost felt good. Real at least. Solid.

Before he could make a move to retaliate, Matthew sucker punched him in the kidney. Seth doubled over, his world all pain.

Dimly, he heard guys pulling Matthew away. "What the hell is your problem? Mad cow disease?" he heard Chad yell. Then Chad was by his side. "You want to lay down or something?"

"Nah. I'm okay. It's okay." Seth slowly straightened up. Coach Austin rushed over and gave him a quick exam.

"Looks like you'll live," the coach said. "But if you see even a drop of blood in your piss, you get yourself to a doctor." Before Seth could answer, Coach Austin was across the court and in Matthew's face.

"You're off the Ravens, Plett. You're lucky I'm not having you expelled," he said, each word coming out hard and clipped.

"Wait. Hey. It's not that big a deal," Seth protested. Benching for a few games, he could see. But kicking Matthew off the team?

"That's not for you to say," the coach answered. He turned back to Matthew. "I want your uniform in my office in five minutes."

"Fine. Of course. You wouldn't want the scout looking at anybody but Golden Boy," Matthew shouted.

"You want me to drive you home?" Chad asked after

Matthew had slammed his way out of the gym.

"I'm okay," Seth said again. Okay except for the fact that all he wanted to do was find a nice quiet place for some quality time with his Pop-Tarts. It's not your fault he got kicked, Seth told himself.

"Man, what happened to Plett?" Chad said. "He's always a butthole. But not like that. He looked insane when he went after you."

Charlie Williams pulled in his driveway, turned off the engine on the ancient Ford he used to get himself to the ferry and back, and just sat there. Staring at his house. He didn't want to go inside. And he was a man who loved coming home. Some of the guys, they wanted to hang out at the Beak, have a drink, shake off the day's bull, but Charlie always went straight home. Stepping through the door, smelling the mix of crayons and the orange air freshener Beth liked, dog hair and the order-in pizza they ended up having at least once a week, the funk of Chad's sneakers— usually left in front of the TV—a little of Beth's Herbal Essence shampoo . . . It was like a bottle of Prozac to him, not that he'd taken Prozac, but the smell was what he thought it would be like, a shot of happiness.

Or at least that's what it had been like for him. Not anymore. Charlie tightened his grip on the steering wheel. He didn't want to go inside.

Get yourself in there, he told himself. You're the dad. You think there's something wrong, it's your job to deal with it. It didn't matter that most of the time he felt like he was still Chad's age, like he hadn't actually grown up and turned into a real adult, like his parents were.

Charlie opened the car door and climbed out. He slammed the door behind him, trying to kill the desire to crawl back inside the safe metal shell. "You're the dad, you deal with it," he told himself again, saying it out loud this time to give it an extra punch.

He marched himself up the driveway and over to his own front door. He swung it open—they didn't bother locking it most of the time, one of the benefits of living on Raven's Point—and faltered. How could he go in there? With that smell. It wasn't strong. There was just a whiff of it, whatever it was—something rotting? something dead?—underneath all the normal home smells he loved.

"Does anyone else smell that?" Charlie called as he forced himself to step into his home. He shut the door behind him and immediately went to the closest window and opened it all the way to the top.

"Smell what?" Beth called from their bedroom.

Charlie didn't answer. How was he supposed to describe that odor? "You're the dad, you deal with it," he muttered. He moved slowly down the front hall, sniffing with every step. It wasn't coming from here . . . . He walked into the living room, automatically swerving left to avoid Barbie's Dream House. The smell was a little stronger in here. Charlie circled the room, sniffing, sniffing.

The freakin' television. That's where it was coming from. It's all the sax and violins. The thought snapped into his head like a mousetrap closing. And he could hear his own father saying the words. It had always cracked Charlie up that his dad wouldn't even use the words "sex" and "violence." It was always "sax" and "violins." His dad was constantly on the lookout for any trace.

And maybe his dad was right. Yesterday Charlie had gotten parental locks set up on the tube. It had suddenly just seemed like something he should do. Like putting a lock on the cabinet with the cleaning supplies in it when you have a little baby.

Charlie forced himself to pull in a long noseful of the air near the TV. His stomach heaved and his throat made that wet clicking sound in the back the way it did when he was about to hurl. The foul stink was definitely coming from this piece of crap.

He grabbed the thirty-two incher in his arms and started for the door. He had to get it away from his family. He was the dad. He had to deal with it. The television jerked in his grasp, like it was alive. Charlie's heart jerked too. Then he realized that he'd forgotten to unplug the thing. Charlie kept on walking. He was stronger than the cord. He felt it pull free from the wall and it gave him a little burst of satisfaction. Yeah, he could deal with this.

Charlie wrangled the front door open and strode out to the curb. Good thing it was garbage night. He dropped the TV onto the pavement, loving the sound when it hit. He turned back toward the house.

But wait. Somebody might see a perfectly good television looking for a home. Somebody might bring the stinking piece of crap into his house. No, he wasn't going to let that happen. Charlie faced the TV. He took aim, pulled back his foot, and kicked the screen. It didn't break. So he kicked it again. And again. Until it shattered. Until he killed it.

Tavia checked the clock. How much longer until she could leave? Fifteen minutes? Half an hour? Or was she supposed to stay until the end, whenever that would be?

"Hey, Tavie!" It was Elijah's dad, acting so jolly, so proud, as if he had brought Elijah out of the coma himself. At least he wasn't looking at her like she was so cold and heartless that she didn't deserve to live. "I think Elijah could use this." He pushed a can of 7UP into her hand.

He's smiling and acting friendly, calling me Tavie because he's trying to get me back with Elijah, Tavia realized. But she obediently walked the soda over to Elijah, who was lying on the sofa surrounded by friends. Everybody stepped back to give her access, but not too far back. They all wanted to see whatever was going to happen next between Tavia and Elijah. Not that anything worth watching had happened so far.

Tavia had shown up at Elijah's welcome home party—how surreal that he was home a week after he'd woken up, even with a full-time live-in nurse—and she'd gone straight over to Elijah. He'd looked at her like she was . . . anybody. The same way he'd looked at Mr. Williams, Elijah's dad's best friend. The same way he'd looked at his sister, Jane. The same way he'd looked at Lucy Choi, even though he'd never liked Lucy.

The same way he was looking at Tavia right now as she handed him his 7UP. The way he'd looked at her in the hospital had made her squirm. It had been too intense, too . . . personal, too I'm seeing your soul. But now Tavia wished

Elijah would look at her like that, really look at her, as if she was someone he loved—someone he had loved, she corrected herself. Because his pleasant, casual thank-you for the soda, with his pleasant smile was turning her body numb. He was the guy who had made her feel things that she'd never known were possible. And now . . .

And now he's treating you the way he's treating all the other people visiting him. That's perfect. That's what you want, Tavia told herself.

Samantha Broder grabbed her upper arm. Tavia could feel the pressure of the grip, but it was like when the dentist was drilling you after a shot of Novocain. You could feel it, but not. "Did you know he was coming?" she whispered.

"Who?" Tavia answered. Then she saw him. Thomas. He was coming straight toward her.

"I thought I'd give you a ride home," Thomas said when he reached Tavia.

"I drove myself," Tavia told him. She realized she'd sounded cold, so she smiled. "But thanks." She might as well use this as an excuse to get going.

But Thomas seemed in no hurry to go. He perched on the edge of the sofa. "Elijah, good to see you home," he said. He reached out and shook Elijah's hand. That was Thomas, kind of old-fashioned. Then Thomas reached over, grabbed Tavia's hand, and pulled her close to him.

Tavia could feel the people surrounding them perk up. Now something interesting was happening. She tried to work her dead-feeling fingers out of Thomas's hand, but he tightened his grip, then leaned down and kissed her knuckles, which was so not a Thomas move.

"I just want you to know that I took good care of Tavia while you were . . . out of school," Thomas continued.

And then there was a beat of silence, one of those silences so powerful you can feel it pressing down on your head. "Yeah," Tavia said, because the silence had to be broken. "Thomas and I started studying together a lot. You know me and my need for many hours of studying."

"Well, we started out studying," Thomas agreed. "But Tavia has other needs too. You understand, Elijah."

Was this Thomas? Sweet Thomas? Thomas who could have his picture in the dictionary under "nice"?

Thomas reached up and began toying with one of her braids. Then he leaned against her, resting his head against one of her breasts. Tavia jerked away. Enough was enough.

"I need to get home to watch *King Lear* on PBS for English," Tavia blurted out, giving the first excuse that came into her head, even though anyone in her English class would know it was a lie. "See you guys at school tomorrow. Well, except you, Elijah, but I'll see you soon."

"Sometimes she just can't wait to get me alone," Thomas said with a smirk. He wrapped his arm around her waist and led her toward the door. Then he stopped abruptly. "One dance before we go."

He didn't wait for her to say yes, he just planted both hands on her butt and started grinding against her. Why doesn't he just go for it and haul me around the room by my hair? Tavia thought wildly. That would show everyone that I'm his, and that's the only reason he's touching me right now.

* * *

Vicki Callison pulled the biggest knife out of the butcher block on her kitchen counter. She liked the feel of it in her hand. The weight. She liked the look of the long, sharp blade. But was it sharp enough to cut through bone? She was sure it was sharp enough to cut through the soft skin of Andrea's unwrinkled neck. Sharp enough to slide through the muscles and tendons, the esophagus and trachea. But the bones. Maybe she'd need to borrow something from the hospital to cut through those.

Hmmm. It would be disastrous to make an attempt and fail. She could drive to the hospital now. She could be back home in less than half an hour. Too long. She needed to do this now.

Vicki laid a dish towel down on the counter. She pressed her left hand flat against it. A little test. That was the answer. She moved her pinky as far away from her other fingers as it would go. Then she brought down the knife.

It does cut through bone, she thought as she watched her blood seep into the dishtowel. But that bone is much smaller than the bone in Andrea's neck.

Handyman Billy gave a twist. He heard the little bones in ratty's neck snap. The sound was nice. Very nice. But it wasn't as nice as the first time he'd heard it.

The bigger the critter, the bigger the crack. That made sense, didn't it? Yes indeedy. And there were lots of critters out there doing things they shouldn't be doing—those nasty garbage-eating raccoons for one. How loud would their crack be?

* * *

Jane dropped a blue recycling bag into the blue trash can. Then she stood there for a minute, just breathing in the night air—slightly tainted by the garbage but still smelling like the ocean. How pathetic is this? she thought. I'd actually rather hang out by the garbage cans than go into my own house.

I should get back. Some kind of referee work might be needed. Jane took in one more breath, then slowly walked to the kitchen door and stepped inside.

"Jane, how do you think Elijah's doing?" her father immediately asked.

"Great. Wow. I mean, he's home. He's walking around. He's the miracle boy of Raven's Point," Jane answered.

"Oh, interesting. Because, your mother, she's not so sure," Jane's dad said.

Jane's mother gave one of her long, tired sighs. "Must you twist every word that comes out of my mouth?"

This was all supposed to change when Elijah got better, Jane thought. She popped a piece of gum into her mouth, anything to stop her teeth from grinding each other down to nubs. Mom and Dad were supposed to be happy again. I was supposed to be able to— I don't even remember what I was supposed to be able to do, Jane realized. Was it all a lie? Was anything really different pre-coma?

Jane let out a sigh that sounded way, way too much like one of her mother's and turned toward the cabinet under the sink to get another garbage bag. The cabinet was white with handprints in primary colors here and there. Jane and Elijah's handprints. Her mother had helped Jane and Elijah make the prints back when Jane was three and Elijah was five. Jane didn't really remember making them, but she'd been told about the day so often that she felt as if she did. Last year, Jane's mom had painted the cabinet dark green.

Lightly Jane touched one of her own little handprints, then she turned around. Her mom, her dad, Elijah, and Jane herself—Jane probably age six—sat at the kitchen table playing Crazy Eights. There was one winter when they'd played almost every night, an ongoing tournament with scores posted on the fridge and much bragging and I'll-get-youing.

Jane-at-six slapped a two down on top of the pile of cards in the center of the table. "That means you have to take two, Dad!" she cried, her grin showing a missing tooth.

"How could you do that to me?" Jane's dad pressed his hand on his heart dramatically. "My own daughter. My own flesh and blood." He took two cards.

"Hey, you told me that she was the runt in that litter of puppies the Williams's dog had," Elijah protested. He studied his cards, shook his head as if he had nothing, then pulled one out of his hand and flipped the two of clubs onto Jane's two of diamonds. "And we all know what that means."

The inside of Jane's nose began to sting. And a hard, salty ball formed in her throat. She slid down the counter and sat on the floor, arms wrapped around her knees.

Jane's mom put her hand over her heart. "How could you do that to me? Your own mother?" she exclaimed. She took two cards. And from her vantage point on the floor, Jane could see her mom's foot in its striped sock give her dad's foot a friendly nudge.

It wasn't all in my imagination, Jane thought. We were happy. At least sometimes. Not Hallmark-card, syrupy happy—from Jane's position on the floor she could also see the booger collection Elijah had going under the seat of his chair—but ordinary happy. God, how long had it been since she'd seen her parents touch each other at all?

"Jane, your turn." Automatically Jane looked over at her mother, who, of course, was speaking to Jane-at-six. But Jane-at-six was looking over at Jane-at-fifteen. Or at least in her direction.

"You're not going to find the card you need over there," Elijah told Jane-at-six.

Jane-at-six drew a card. Then she twisted around in her chair and stared at the older Jane again. Does she see me? Jane-at-fifteen thought.

"Mom, there's something in here," younger Jane announced.

She doesn't see me—at least not yet, Jane-at-fifteen realized. But she feels me. That's the last thing she—I—need. Seeing ghosts or whatever she'd think I am.

Jane turned her back on her family, wishing she could watch them for just a few more seconds. She stared at the bright handprints on the cabinet. Green, she thought. Nothing changed. She'd never actually made herself come out of one of her . . . visions before. She had no clue what she was supposed to do. Green, she thought again. And she felt something shift in her brain.

Then she was back. Back in almost the last place she wanted to be.

"All I said was that I thought he seemed a little remote," Jane's mother told Jane's dad. Clearly Jane hadn't missed any time in the present.

"I don't find him remote in the least. If you do, maybe you should ask yourself why," Jane's father said, his voice getting lower and softer the way it always did when he was angry. "Could it be that your son senses you gave up on him long ago?"

Fast as lightning, Jane's mother's hand went up, and she slapped Jane's father across the face, hard. The sound seemed to reverberate through the kitchen. Jane watched a red handprint come up on her dad's cheek as the skin around it went white.

Then slowly, his hand came up.

"Dad, no!" Jane cried. This was so wrong. Her parents never got violent with each other. Never.

She took a step to get between her parents. Too late. With a crack, her father's palm hit her mother's face.

Chapter 5

Burn It Up, Burn It Down

The phone was ringing when Tavia got home from school. She ran to the kitchen and grabbed it. "You did it with the white boy, didn't you?" a husky voice asked. "You did it with him, but I'm not good enough for you. Is that it, Tavia? I'm not good enough for you?"

"Thomas?" Tavia exclaimed.

The only answer was a click and then the dial tone. But it was him. It hadn't sounded like him. But it was.

I left the door unlocked, she thought. What if Thomas was calling on his cell? What if he's right outside? Tavia rushed to the front door and locked it. She put on the chain, a ridiculous, flimsy thing—the screws that held it to the wall would pull free in seconds if somebody really wanted in. But those few seconds could give her enough time to call nine-one-one.

Okay, now that's overdramatic, she told herself. There

wasn't going to be any need for the police. She walked to the nearest window, closed it, locked it, double-checked the lock. When she completed a circuit of the house, she programmed nine-one-one into the phone's speed dial.

"You're being silly," she said aloud. "Thomas isn't going to come busting in here." Yet here she was, locking all the windows, wishing her parents would both get home early from work so she wouldn't be alone.

Tavia wandered into her room and put on her favorite Tori Amos CD. *What if he's in the house already?* The thought erupted in Tavia's head. *He wasn't in school today. What if he broke in here after my parents and I left and is waiting for me?* Her heart started thrashing around in her chest, as if it were trying to free itself.

Okay, now you've really become delusional, Tavia told herself as she began to search the house. You aren't starring in *Halloween Part 17.* But she continued moving from room to room, checking every possible hiding place. Parents' closet. Under their bed. In their shower. In the bathtub of the hall bathroom. In the linen closet. In the garage. The whole place was still and quiet, except for the sound of Tori Amos singing.

Tavia returned to her bedroom. Checked her closet. Stretched out on her stomach and checked under her bed. Something was under there. Not Thomas. Just a box. But the sight of it was like the cut of a knife.

Leave it there, Tavia thought. But her hands, traitors, were already reaching for it. She pulled it toward her, her fingers squeaking against the packing tape wrapped around every inch of the box. She hadn't planned to ever open the box again. She couldn't bring herself to throw it away, but she hadn't planned to look inside. That's why she'd used a whole roll of packing tape to keep it closed.

Tavia placed the box on her bed, then retrieved a pair of scissors from her desk. She ran one of the blades over the box's center seam. It took several passes to cut through all the layers of tape. She repeated the process on the two short ends of the box top, then, not allowing herself a moment to think, she opened the box. The first thing she saw was a layer of shredded newspaper.

No, god, it was the grass skirt Elijah had made for her out of long strips of newspaper. How could she have forgotten about it for even an instant? They'd been going out for about a year. It was one of the wettest, coldest Raven's Point winters ever. Tavia had felt as if it were never going to end. She'd been longing to see even a few rays of sunshine.

"Step. Another step. One more," Elijah coached. "And we're here." He took off Tavia's blindfold. Elijah was now wearing a grass skirt made of long strips of newspaper stapled to a pair of boxers. Tavia was wearing one also. So that was what Elijah had slid up her body as soon as he'd gotten her blindfolded.

"This is amazing," she told him. Two beach towels lay in the middle of the basement along with a couple pairs of sunglasses, a half-deflated beach ball, a bunch of canister candles, and an insane number of plastic flowers.

"Welcome to Hawaii! Can you smell the coconuts? Can you hear the ukuleles?" Elijah held up one hand. "Wait. Don't answer that." Moving like a big grasshopper he leapt over to the CD player next to the beach blankets,

punched a button, then leapt back to her. "Can you hear the ukuleles?" he asked again.

She could. And a man singing "Somewhere over the rainbow" in a high, sweet voice. "The guy's Hawaiian. Really," Elijah told her. "And now, we hula!" He started waving his arms and wriggling his hips.

Tavia laughed, the sound tickling as it came out, like soda fizz in her throat. "You aren't dancing," Elijah said.

"I don't know how to hula," Tavia answered, stalling. How did Elijah do it? Just completely let go and make a fool of himself? And make her laugh. And make her want to kiss him a million times?

"I'll teach you. The first thing you have to know is that in the hula every motion has a meaning," he lectured, slipping into his imitation of their homeroom teacher. "For example." Elijah crossed his hands over his heart and gave his pelvis a double jerk. "This means 'I love you.'"

He stopped dancing. And he stepped up to her and ran his fingers down her cheek. "I love you, Tavia."

He'd been the brave one, the first one to actually say the words aloud.

Tavia gently folded the grass skirt and set it aside. I shouldn't be doing this, she thought. There was a reason I taped up the box so tight.

She'd known it would hurt. And it did. If she'd used the scissors to stab herself in the heart it couldn't hurt more.

Pretend you've just moved in to your first apartment, Tavia told herself. Pretend you just got a fabulous job as a law clerk. You found this box in your storage unit and decided to look inside. And you have all these great memories of your first boyfriend. But that was a long time ago. No one ends up with their first love.

First love. Would she ever love anybody the way she'd loved Elijah? Tavia took one of the canister candles from that day in Hawaii out of the box and lit it. The sweet smell of fake coconut filled the room.

What are you doing? she asked herself. Just tape the box back up. Tape it up tight. Open it years from now. But her hands took control again. They reached into the box—and pulled out a candy necklace. Tavia'd worn it every day, even when she went running, until her sweat had started to eat away at the candy. Elijah had given it to her after a fight.

"*Aren't you ever serious,*" *Tavia hissed, trying to keep her voice at library level.* "*You can't just graduate, show up at a college, and go 'here I am, where do I sign up?' You're supposed to be working on your extracurricular activities. Basketball's great. But it's not like you're recruitment material. You need more.*"

"*The only extracurricular activity I'm interested in is getting you alone,*" *Elijah interrupted.*

"*Then you're a fool.*"

Tavia dove back into the box again. A valentine made out of a paper plate, the kind you made in kindergarten. Unless you were Elijah, who was fourteen at the time.

She quickly put it aside. The fight was easier to remember than the day Elijah gave her the valentine. She took the next item out of the box. The list. God, the list. She forced herself to unfold the piece of ordinary looseleaf binder paper. Her vision blurred with tears, but she blinked them away and read the reasons she'd had for breaking up with Elijah:

1. We would have broken up anyway, when we both went off to college.

2. I know you wouldn't want me to spend my life sitting by your bed. If the situation were reversed, I'd want you to break up with me.

3. My parents never wanted me to be so serious with a guy while I was in high school.

4. Your mother thinks it's the right thing to do.

5. I need all my time and energy to keep my grades up, get myself elected to the school council, and train for the Boston marathon.

Tavia refolded the list. I forgot one, she thought. I forgot the most important reason—that I was connected to Elijah in so many ways I was going into the coma right along with him. It was dangerous to care about someone like that, she knew that now. She'd learned.

Tape. She needed tape. It was a waste of time going through all this stuff now. Her college essay wouldn't write itself. And it needed to be perfect. Tavia started for her desk, then turned back toward the box. She snatched up the grass skirt and shoved it inside. She thrust in the valentine, not caring if it got folded.

She grabbed the candle. For some reason the warmth of the glass canister surprised her. Of course it was warm. Candle. Warm. But she closed her eyes and cradled it in her hands as if it were alive, letting the warmth soak into her hands and travel through her body.

Her skin grew hotter. Uncomfortably hot. Blistering. She could actually hear it crackling, like bacon in a skillet.

Smoke invaded her nostrils, bringing with it the smell of meat, burning meat. Not meat. Her skin. Her flesh. She was on fire. "No!" she shouted.

The sound of her own voice jolted her out of her . . . what should it be called, trance? She opened her eyes and looked down at the tiny candle flame. It was nothing to be afraid of. But she blew it out quickly.

Handyman Billy was right. The bigger the critter, the bigger the crack. But a crack was fast. The raccoon had been alive. Now it was limp in his hands. Way too fast. Raccoons were pests. They didn't deserve a fast death. They should have to suffer first after all the nuisance they'd caused. Billy would think on that.

Seth was the first one out of the showers and the first one out of the locker room after practice. He half expected Matthew to be waiting for him, even though Matthew hadn't been in school that day. Not that Seth would care if Matthew were waiting. Seth could take care of himself—at least against anything that was still alive. Matthew had caught him by surprise with that punch on the court, true. But Matthew wouldn't get lucky like that a second time.

Need my geometry book, Seth realized. He reversed direction and headed toward his locker. He almost missed her. She was sitting on the bench next to the drinking fountain, so quiet and still she was almost invisible. "Jane, hey."

She jumped, her binder almost falling off her lap, her purple pen rolling across the linoleum floor. Seth picked up the pen and carried it to her. "Didn't mean to scare you," he told her.

"You didn't," she answered. "Okay, I'm lying," she added quickly, before he had a chance to respond. "You did scare me a little. But it's not your fault. I've been jumpy lately."

"Me too," Seth admitted. He sat down next to her. He hadn't been planning to. But there was something about the girl. He hardly knew her, but when he got close to her, he felt . . . just calmer. Like the world was a place that might actually make sense.

"Jumpy, like, jumping for the basket? Like slam dunk?" Jane asked. She unzipped the little plastic compartment hooked into her binder and stuck the pen inside.

Seth laughed. "No. I meant what you meant. Edgy jumpy."

"'Cause of the scout?" Jane asked. The harsh fluorescent bulbs created a semicircle of light around her part. He liked her hair, how it was all fluffy instead of straight and sleek. His fingers would feel so warm burrowing in there.

What the hell was he thinking? He'd spoken to Jane twice and now he was imagining his hands in her hair? "The scout, yeah," Seth answered. That was a nice, normal thing to be edgy about. He certainly wasn't going to tell her he was jumpy because a few days ago he'd seen the boy he'd killed, and since then had seen a couple of other dead guys. Or maybe just one more if the mouth screaming in the bathroom belonged to the naked old man wandering on the basketball court. "What about you?"

"The same," Jane answered. She unzipped the plastic pencil holder, then zipped it again.

Seth leaned back against the cool cinder block wall. "You're nervous about the scout?"

"Okay, that was stupid. Really stupid. I didn't mean to say that," Jane answered. She unzipped the pencil holder again, and Seth noticed that her fingernails were bitten down to the quick. She really was knotted up about something.

"So what did you mean to say?" Seth asked. He stretched his legs out in front of him, his muscles feeling loose and warm.

"I meant to say something normal sounding, like I'm worried about the French test I have tomorrow." Jane ran her fingers through her fluffy light brown hair, and Seth could almost feel it wrapped around his own hands.

"Well, since you didn't, you now have to tell me the real deal. It's a rule." Jane reached for the zipper on the pencil holder again, and Seth shut her binder so she couldn't get at it. Jane looked up at him, startled. "Are your eyes green or brown?" Seth asked. I'm a moron, he thought.

Jane blinked. "Hazel. But sometimes they look more green or more brown depending on what I'm wearing. Or if I eat a lot of sugar, I think it makes them look greener. The jealousy thing, though—haven't noticed an effect."

"They're pretty," Seth told her. Seventeen years old, and it was the first time he'd said anything like that to a girl. He'd basically stayed away from the whole guy/girl world, because he didn't think there were many girls out there who'd want to start something up with a murderer. There were a few, he guessed—you heard about them writing to serial killers in prison. But those kinds of girls weren't the kind of girls Seth had any desire to get to know.

"Um, thanks," Jane said. And she blushed, actually

blushed. He could see the color between every freckle on her face.

Seth was saved from having to figure out what to say next by a squeal of metal. A second later, the janitor rounded the corner pushing a mop bucket with at least a couple of rusty wheels. "I'm gonna be locking up soon."

Jane jumped to her feet. "I should get home."

"Me too." So were they supposed to walk out together? Or should he let her go on ahead? He took a couple of slow steps, letting her decide. She fell into step beside him. "So don't think you're getting out of answering the question. Why are you jumpy?"

"I don't know. I mean, I do, but it's stupid," Jane said in a rush. "I'm actually stressed because my brother's home, which is stupid, because that's pretty much the best thing that's happened to me ever. But my parents keep fighting. And—"

Jane clamped her teeth down on her bottom lip. Seth couldn't stop looking at the little indentation she was making. Her bottom lip was fuller than her top one. Stop, he told himself. She's trying to tell you something important and you're zoning out, staring at her mouth. "And?" he prompted.

"And now you know why I should have just said I was nervous about a French test," Jane answered. "You don't need all that garbage dumped on you."

They reached the double glass doors of the main entrance. Seth got there first and held a door open for Jane. Should he ask if she wanted a ride home? It would be kind of rude not to. Except she probably wouldn't want to get on even a bus with him if she knew the truth about him. He adjusted his backpack on his shoulder, stalling. "I forgot to get my geometry book," he burst out. "Do you want to wait a minute? I could give you a ride if you want. It's pretty cold."

"That would . . . No, I should get home. It's not very far. But thanks." Jane gave him a little wave and rushed away.

Seth turned around and started for his locker. He'd only been separated from Jane for a few seconds, but he could feel the vertebrae of his spine moving closer together, tightening up. How could she— His sneaker slid across something wet. He looked down. And saw blood.

The puddle of blood began to pulse. Seth backed away an instant before it shot up in a geyser. Arms punched out from the liquid column. A head formed. The bottom of the column split into legs. And the old man was standing in front of him.

Seth ran. He heard wet footsteps right behind him, but he didn't look back. All he had to do was get to the parking lot, get to his car. Grateful for every hour of training, Seth pushed himself to the limit. He cut across the school's front lawn, rounded the corner. His eyes went immediately to his car, almost alone in the lot.

A girl in a long black dress, pregnant, stood blocking the driver's-side door. She held a torch in one hand. Seth responded the way he would on the court. He pivoted, and kept running. A flash of movement to his right told him the old man was still on him.

Seth stayed on the main street. There weren't many

people out. He should have headed toward the Beak. That place was always crowded, even out of the tourist season. Seth shot a glance over his shoulder. The old man was about five paces behind. The girl just a few steps behind him. What did they want? What in holy hell did they want?

Who gives a crap? Seth thought. Whatever they want, they can get it from someone else. One more block and the little row of shops would end. A block after that and the road turned to dirt path and led straight up to the point. That was the last place he wanted to go. He'd be cornered on the edge of the cliff. Ghosts in one direction. Long drop to the ocean—and the rocks—in the other.

Gotta get off this street, he told himself. He feinted right, then charged left. There was a church near the end of Holly Street. He could go there. They wouldn't be able to follow. Would they?

Christ. Holly Street was blocked off by a man with an axe; a boy with a noose; three men with seaweed twined in their wet hair; and a little girl, a little girl holding, Christ, a dead baby. All of them wearing clothes that looked like they came from hundreds of years ago.

Seth kept running straight. He didn't have any other option. Maybe when he hit the top of the cliff he could scramble down to the ocean. There weren't many hand-holds and it was steep as hell, but maybe he had a shot. He felt the ground under his sneakers turn from asphalt to dirt. His lungs protested as Seth struggled not to lose a second of speed starting up the incline.

He could hear them behind him. There might be more

of them now. It sounded like a crowd. A lynch mob. Seth locked his eyes on the oak tree at the top of the cliff and kept running. When he got there . . . When he got there he'd figure something out.

The incline leveled off. He'd reached the top of the cliff faster than he'd thought. He could hear the waves crashing onto the rocks. He could hear the footsteps pounding behind him.

Seth whirled to face the ghosts. To see how close they were. Four teenagers had joined the group. They broke free from the others and ran toward him. As they ran, they burst into flames. Then they were on him. Lighting his shirt. His pants. His hair. It was as if he'd been doused in gasoline. All he could see was flames. They were burning him alive.

"You're the dad, you have to deal with it," Charlie Williams chanted as he kicked through the computer monitor. He left the dead computer on the curb and returned to the house. Satisfied he'd done his duty.

But the stench was still there. Overpowering all the good smells of his home—the crayons and his wife's shampoo and the dog hair. "Still more sax and violins," he muttered. But where? Charlie gave a sniff. There was definitely something rotten in the living room. His eyes shifted from the couch to the chairs to the coffee table to the bookshelf.

The books. Yes. Who knew what was inside some of them? Charlie launched himself at the bookcase. He didn't have time to decide which books were the stinkers. He knocked the bookcase to the ground. Now all he needed was his can of lighter fluid. That and a match. He was the dad. He'd deal with it.

Vicki Callison stood in the surgical supply room. It was a good thing to work in the hospital, with all these beautiful cutting things. Surely many of them could cut through the bones of Andrea's neck. All Vicki had to do was pick out her favorite.

She selected a saw with a circular blade not much bigger than the lid of a soup can. Cunning little thing. She switched it on. The blade spun so fast she couldn't see the individual teeth. So convenient. Anyone could use something like this. You wouldn't need any strength at all to cut through bone with this.

Still, it was probably better to be absolutely sure. Vicki opened a box of gauze pads. She laid several on an empty shelf, then she positioned her hand on top of them. And brought the whirring blade down on her wrist.

Seth ran his fingers over his face, his hair. His skin was smooth. His hair hadn't been singed off his head. But he had felt his bones turning molten. He'd felt his tongue fuse to the roof of his mouth.

"You want my opinion—not that you're asking—they weren't trying to set you on fire."

Seth whipped his head to the left, and there was Terry Rheingold trudging down the hill beside him.

"What?" Seth snapped.

Terry shrugged. "I just didn't get the vibe that they wanted to hurt you."

"What makes you think—" Seth shook his head. "I'm doing it again. Talking to you like you're actually here."

"Who else are you going to talk about this stuff to?" Terry asked. "I'll tell you—nobody. Unless you want them to think you're crazy."

"Fine. Okay. Whatever." Seth was so flipped that he didn't really care all that much. And those ghosts that had chased him up the hill—pretty damn real seeming. Maybe Terry was real too. "So what do you think they wanted?"

Terry shrugged. "Just 'cause I'm dead and they're dead doesn't mean I can read their minds or anything. I'm just telling you what it seemed like to me." He kicked a rock in his path. His foot went through it. "So are you gonna ask out that girl Jane or what?"

"What?" How did Jane come into this conversation?

"What?" Terry repeated, imitating Seth's shocked tone. "You know you want to."

Seth considered it for half a second. No. "A girl like Jane wouldn't—"

"Wouldn't want to go out with a cold-blooded killer." Terry snorted. "You're not exactly Hannibal the Cannibal, you know. And don't you think it would be nice to get laid while you're still young enough to get it up?"

"I had a hamburger with the girl and you're talking about getting laid?" Seth protested.

"What I'm talking about is you using me as an excuse," Terry shot back. "Forget getting laid. You've never even kissed a girl. You want to be a huge wuss? Fine. But stop blaming it on me."

And he was gone.

"Terry?" Seth turned in a slow circle. "Are you still there? Are you screwing with me?"

There was no answer.

"Good. My mental health is returning," Seth muttered. But he felt more alone than ever.

Jane didn't allow herself one moment to grab a snack. She didn't even pop a piece of gum, although of course her teeth were squeaking against each other. She went straight up the stairs and down the hall. A "Welcome Home" banner made by the Brownie troop hung on the open door of Elijah's room.

Elijah's room. It so didn't seem like Elijah's room anymore. He was only a year and a half older than he was when he slept in here every night, but now he seemed too big for the single bed, definitely too old for the mobile of the solar system that he'd made in the sixth grade. Yeah, he'd been too old for it at sixteen too, but he'd still liked it. Now he probably thought it was trash.

Nervously, she switched the rolled up poster from one hand to the other, the plastic wrapping slick from the sweat that kept popping up between her fingers. This was the dumbest present. It didn't fit Elijah any better than the mobile did. "Hey," she said as she stepped inside.

Marti Neemy, Elijah's nurse looked up from her magazine. She smiled at Jane. "I'll be in the kitchen if you need me," Marti announced as she headed out the bedroom door. Jane wished she'd stayed. But she couldn't say "please don't leave because I don't want to be alone with my own brother."

"Hey, Elijah," Jane said. He didn't turn away from his

computer, but she sat down on his bed as if he'd invited her. "Catching up on current events?"

He didn't answer. Mom was being generous when she called him remote, Jane thought. *What does Dad see when he looks at him? How can he think that Elijah is fine?*

Of course, when he asked you what you thought of Elijah, you went into cheerleader mode—"Oh, Dad, he's just an M-I-R-A-C-L-E!!"

"I got you something." Jane reached out and tapped Elijah on the shoulder with the rolled-up poster. He spun his desk chair around so fast it made her gasp. "It's no big thing. Don't get your hopes up." She handed him the poster.

He stared down at it for a moment, eyes blank. Then he tore off the wrapping. *God, his fingernails are long,* Jane thought. *They must have kept them clipped in the hospital and Marti hasn't noticed how out of control they are. His hair's long, too. I can't believe it's grown that much since he got out of the hospital.*

Elijah unrolled the poster, blocking his face. Then something amazing happened—he laughed. Jane laughed too. She always started to laugh when Elijah laughed. "Duckies? You got me duckies?" Elijah asked.

"Yeah. I told you not to get your hopes up. I was in the poster place and I saw it and I remembered how we both used to love the ducks, even though that was like a million years ago, and so I bought it." Jane didn't mention the other reason she bought it. Over the picture of the little ducklings breaking out of their eggs were the words "Arise, go forth, and conquer." Somehow, dorky as it was, she just had to get the poster for Elijah when she read those words. It was what she wanted for him, what she wanted to give him.

"Quanks, Quane," Elijah said, using the quacking duck language they'd spoken when they were kids.

"You're quelcome," Jane quacked back. If flowers had started sprouting out of her skin she wouldn't have been surprised. That's how good she felt. Elijah had quacked for her. "Quy quid . . . "

Jane let her words trail off. The blankness, the *remoteness*, was back. Elijah was looking at her—at least his eyes were pointed at her. But they could have been two buttons stuck in his head. There was no life there. Nobody home.

Is it always going to be like this? she wondered. Will Elijah be able to come out only for a few seconds at a time forever? Will he still be like this in a year? Two? If he was, Jane couldn't imagine what her family would be like. "What's going to happen to us?" she whispered.

Jane stood up, took a step, and fell. Her legs and arms flailed, searching for the ground. Then she hit. Not the floor of Elijah's bedroom. Or even the floor of the living room below. She'd landed in a pile of . . . Jane reached out and rubbed the soft black stuff between her fingers. Ash. She was in a pile of ash.

She shoved herself to her knees and stared around. All she could see was blackness. She could hear the ocean. And the sound of her own breathing, but that was it. Slowly she stood. She took a few steps, her feet sinking deep into the ash. Her eyes adjusted to the darkness, and she realized that there truly was nothing surrounding her. No houses, no trees. Nothing.

Had everything burned? Is that where the ashes had

come from? Jane turned in a slow circle, dizzy, not from the motion, but from the endless destruction that lay around her.

It's one of my time shifts, she thought. I touched the plaque in the hospital and I went back to when the hospital was new. Seth read the year the drive-through was founded off the menu, and I went back to that year.

Okay, okay. Jane knotted her hands together. So, maybe I'm back in, like, prehistoric times before anything was built on the island. In a second, I'll shift back. Like I did the other times. I'll be home. And everything will be all right. Well, not all right but—

Another thought exploded in Jane's brain. There'd been no trigger this time. The last time this had happened she'd wondered if her family had ever been happy. And it was like the time shift had answered her question. She'd gone back to a time when her family was having fun together.

Jane's breath started to come in harsh pants. She could feel herself sucking down flakes of the ash, but she couldn't slow her breathing. Maybe this time shift had been an answer to a question too. But this time the question had been about the future.

Chapter 6

The Past Isn't Past

"Seth, got a surprise for you." A basketball flew out of the darkness and hit Seth on the shoulder.

A surprise, Seth thought. Greaaat. 'Cause those ghosts setting me on fire, that was pretty boring.

"You ready?" Seth's dad called.

"Sure. Can't wait," Seth answered. What else was there to say—Dad, can it wait until tomorrow because some ghosts kinda freaked me out?

"Okay. Here we go. One, two, and three," Seth's father called. An instant later the driveway was flooded with light. "Professional court-quality lighting. Thought you might need to get in some night practice." He held out his hands, waiting.

Seth threw his dad the ball. "Cool. Thanks."

"So how about a game of horse before dinner?" His dad dribbled the ball, then shot from where he stood. *Swish*. He snagged the ball off the ground and passed it to Seth.

No biggie. A little game. I can do this, Seth thought. He dropped his backpack and walked over to the spot his dad had thrown from, took aim, and let the ball fly. It bounced off the rim.

"That's an *H* for you," Seth's dad announced. He didn't sound happy about it. Usually Seth's dad loved to win. Seth's father scooped the ball up and chose a spot to the right of the hoop. Swish. "Your turn."

Seth grabbed the ball and got into position. He adjusted his grip on the pebbly rubber, took aim, threw. And didn't even manage to get some rim. The ball bounced off the backboard, then bounced off down the driveway and into the street.

"That's an *O* for you," his dad said, staring after the ball. Seth realized his father was waiting for him to run and get it. He was relieved to have a few seconds out of the driveway's bright lights. But he knew he'd only piss his dad off further—'cause it was clear he was pissed now—if he didn't hustle. He snatched the ball and trotted it back up the driveway, then tossed it to his dad.

His dad started to dribble. In the bright light, Seth could see every line on his father's face. Yeah, he was definitely pissed off. Those creases alongside his mouth had tightened and a furrow had appeared between his eyebrows.

"These lights are gonna be a huge help," Seth said quickly. Maybe he hadn't sounded happy enough about them. And they probably cost some bucks. His dad was one of those buy-the-best-or-don't-bother guys.

"It's not going to happen again, is it?" Seth's dad asked, still dribbling.

"What?" Seth replied, his eyes following the ball so he didn't have to look at his dad's face.

"You just missed two cake shots. Where's your concentration?" His father stopped dribbling and threw the ball. Swish. "There's no excuse for flubbing a shot when you're standing perfectly still and have time to take aim, for crying out loud."

This was about missing a couple of shots, for chrissakes? What was his dad's problem? Seth grabbed the ball, stalked over to position on the driveway. He didn't take time to aim. And he bounced the ball right off the friggin' rim again. Seth turned around to retrieve it, but his father caught him by the arm, forcing Seth to stop and face him.

"I'm not trying to be a jerk," his father told him. "It's just that this is a crucial time for you, Seth. You need to be in top form. I'd hate to see a repeat of what happened in Sacramento, that's all."

"That's not gonna happen," Seth promised. "I've been doing fine at practice."

"You were doing more than fine at practice then too," his father answered. "Then at the game . . . " He let his words trail off. Neither of them needed to be reminded of the final game of the season at Seth's old school. Seth had missed two free throws in a row, which ended the game. And that was after numerous other screwups.

"Look, everyone has a bad night, but it was almost like you wanted to lose," Seth's dad said.

All those banners with his name on them. The cheerleaders had made up a whole cheer about him. The coach had started out the game by saying to pass to Seth, pass to

Seth whenever possible. The giant had been squeezing with both hands that night. And the two boxes of cinnamon Pop-Tarts he'd scarfed down at halftime hadn't helped him any.

"I didn't want to lose," Seth muttered. But he had wanted people to stop looking at him like he was some kind of hero. No one should ever look at him like that.

"Then what's the deal tonight?" his father asked.

"I . . . I have a lot going on." Seth tried to come up with something that would satisfy his dad. The truth—the whole ghost thing—wasn't going to work for him here. "There's this paper I'm supposed to have started writing, and a test in geometry tomorrow," Seth continued.

"You've never had a problem—"

The front door swung open. "Dinner, you guys," his mom called out.

"I should get the ball." Seth was halfway down the driveway before the sentence was out of his mouth. By the time he'd picked up the ball and turned back around, his dad had disappeared inside.

Seth picked up his backpack and followed him. He shoved the ball in the front hall closet, then headed into the kitchen. "Okay if I eat in my room?" he asked, picking up his plate. "I need to do some research on the net for that paper I'm writing."

"We'll miss you," his mother said with a smile, "but I suppose school has to come first."

On the way to his room, he made a pit stop in the bathroom. He double-checked to make sure the door was locked, then he pulled his box of Pop-Tarts out of his backpack. Carrying the tarts around with him all the time was macho bullcrap. Because then anytime he felt like eating one—like he did now—there they were. He ripped open the box, then ripped open the first silver package his fingers touched. He flipped open the lid of the toilet with his foot, then crumbled the Pop-Tarts to bits over the Ty-D-Bowl-blue water. Flushed. And repeated until the Pop-Tarts were gone. Then he washed his hands until there wasn't a speck of pastry or sugary goo left on his skin and continued to his room.

He was online in half a second. His parents had gotten him a DSL line for his 'puter. He got himself to Google and typed in "ghosts." Christ. He'd be wearin' Depends before he got through all these entries. Seth skimmed the list. The word "communication" caught his eye. He double clicked.

"Okay, yeah. This is what I need," he muttered. He'd lucked onto a great site, really organized. There was even a section on why ghosts appeared to humans. He grabbed a sheet of paper and a pen, and started taking notes. There wasn't a ton to write. At least according to this Web site, ghosts were pretty basic.

They appear if they haven't been buried properly, he wrote. Huh. There'd been, he thought, maybe twelve of them surrounding him on the point. Could all have been buried in some messed-up way—left in the woods or something? If they had wanted him to find their bodies and bury them, they'd asked him in a pretty stupid way. Being set on fire didn't make anybody feel like doing favors. Unless maybe they were trying to tell him they wanted to be cremated? That didn't make much sense.

They appear if they have an undone task, he wrote. *For example, a ghost might be trying to communicate the presence of a hidden will.* Again, pretty bizarre way to ask for help finishing up undone business, Seth thought.

They come to announce a death. Oh, very nice. 'Cause if I'm going to die by being burned alive, I'm really happy I'll be able to experience it twice, he thought. But maybe if that was the deal, he could stop it somehow. The weird thing was—well, there were many weird things—but one of the weird things was that the ghosts had all been wearing old-fashioned clothes. Except the naked dude. They'd looked like Pilgrims or something. Why would a bunch of people from hundreds of years ago be worried about him?

They come to exact vengeance, Seth wrote. Torching someone was a good way to get even, he thought. But, again, the old-fashioned clothes thing. Why would some Pilgrims, or whatever they were, want to set him on fire?

Charlie Williams flicked on the electric dog clippers. Good. Still working. He walked down the hall and stopped in the doorway of Alexis's room. His daughter was sitting on the floor, her head bent over her coloring book as she carefully used a purple crayon on a cloud. Her long, shiny blond hair hung all the way down her back.

She was just a little girl. The stink shouldn't be coming from her. But it was. Sax. The smell of sax was pulsing off her. It was the hair. He was almost sure it was that long, blond hair.

He hesitated for a moment longer, watching Alexis trade the purple crayon for a tangerine-colored one. You're the dad, you have to deal with it, Charlie told himself. Then he marched himself over to Alexis.

"Hi, Daddy," she said.

He couldn't choke out a word. He got on his knees behind her and wrapped one arm around her waist. With his free hand he flipped on the clippers. Alexis screamed when the cold metal tangled in her hair. She twisted from side to side, trying to escape from him. But he held her tight. Until her hair, her goldy locks—that's what he used to call them—lay all over the floor, until only bristles were left on Alexis's head.

"Get me a beer, will you?" Bob Plett asked.

Wouldn't hurt you to walk from the sofa to the fridge once in a while, you fat lump of crap, Matthew thought. But he got up and headed into the kitchen.

McFadden's dad probably got his own beer. Matthew'd seen him around. The guy showed up at every game and even hit practice once in a while. And he definitely looked like he did some running, maybe lifted weights. Probably even played some one-on-one with Seth.

Matthew grabbed a beer from the cardboard box. He popped the top—even that was too much effort for the old man. Having a dad who could stand up without grunting, wonder what that would be like? he thought. If I'd been handed a basketball at birth the way I'm sure wonder boy McFadden was, I'm sure—

"What's taking you?" his dad shouted.

Matthew tilted back his head and drained half his dad's beer with one long gulping swallow. Wonder what would happen if I replaced what I drank with Liquid Plumr? he thought.

Tavia pulled on her sweats and her running shoes. The backs of her hands were smooth and unblemished. Tavia couldn't stop staring at them as she tied her shoelaces. Yesterday, she'd felt the skin crack open. She'd smelled her flesh burn.

Obviously, it was a dream, she told herself. Except that you were awake.

The run would help her. The cool air would clean out her head, and the exercise would work some of the tension out of her body. Tavia grabbed her Walkman, put it on, and hit Play. The sound of Beth Orton's voice filled her ears. It wasn't really good running music. But *NSYNC only reminded her of Elijah now, and she needed a break from thinking about him. She needed a break from thinking about almost everything.

Tavia stepped out into the foggy morning. She propped one leg up on the porch railing and bent over it, savoring the stretch in her back and leg. She wrapped her hands around her foot and deepened the stretch, pressing her cheek against her leg, focusing on the physical sensations, trying to let them become her whole world.

Stretches completed, she began to run, looking forward to the hill. But the instant she reached the dirt path, a pair of hands spun her around. She found herself staring up at Thomas, conscious for the first time of how much taller he was, how much bigger his hands were.

Keep it light, she ordered herself. "Thomas, did you

decide you were ready for the challenge of the hill?"

"I'm ready for you to tell me the truth," Thomas answered, digging his fingers into her flesh. "You slept with the white boy, didn't you?"

"That's none of your business," Tavia told him. Wrong answer, she thought when she saw Thomas's mouth tighten with anger.

"It's my business if you slept with the white boy, when you haven't given it up for me," Thomas shot back. "You want to be with somebody white. Your mother got herself a white man— why shouldn't you? That's it, isn't it?"

He's lost it, she thought. He's totally gone.

Tavia knew she could run faster than Thomas. But what good would that do? Even if she pulled away from him, he was blocking the way back into town. And the path dead-ended at the top of the point. Gotta do something. Gotta do *something*.

"Thomas, you know I love you, right?" Tavia said, hoping she sounded sincere. "I haven't said it, because, well, you haven't said it to me. But I do love you. And I assumed we'd—" Tavia struggled to get the words out without gagging. "That we'd make love sometime soon. I thought you probably had something special planned. Something romantic. You're so sweet that way."

Believe it. Please be stupid enough to believe it.

Thomas relaxed his grip on her shoulders. He slid his hands down her arms. "I think this spot right here is pretty romantic," he said. Then his lips were on hers, his tongue forcing its way into her mouth.

Tavia twisted her head away. "Help!" she screamed.

Although no one was ever out on the path this early. "Help!" she screamed again.

A growl came from behind Thomas. Over his shoulder she saw the first two dogs that had shown up on her run days ago. They looked almost like completely different animals. Instead of cuddly, feral. Instead of friendly, fearsome.

Still growling, the dogs flanked Tavia, eyes locked on Thomas. "They won't hurt you if you leave now," she told him. "Just leave now." Thomas stared at her for a long moment, his expression a mix of anger, fear, and pain, then he turned and walked away. "Stay with me," she ordered the dogs. "Don't you move." They obeyed.

When Thomas was out of sight, Tavia turned and started up the hill. She needed to run, run fast, now. Her long strides ate up the ground. Harder, harder, harder, she urged herself.

Instead, she slowed down. Because the squirrels in the nearest tree were staring at her. A possum had stopped dead on the path ahead of her. It was staring too.

"What?" Tavia screamed, the word ripping her throat on the way out. "What do you want? Why is this happening to me?"

As if in answer, she heard the sound of dozens of bird wings flapping. No, hundreds. The wings created a breeze she could feel against her face, a warm breeze filled with that weird powdery scent birds seemed to have.

The flapping grew louder. The breeze grew stronger. Then the birds were on her. Their claws and beaks grabbed her sweat clothes, her shoes, even tangled in her hair. On what seemed like an unspoken signal, the birds began to flap in unison.

And Tavia's feet left the ground. Her body went limp. She couldn't struggle. Her brain had no control over her body anymore.

The birds carried her into the sky, up and up, until she could see the whole island of Raven's Point at once, the ocean stretching out around it. Pretty, she thought, with no emotion. Too much had happened today. She'd just shut down, she guessed.

Look, the cemetery, she thought. As if she was watching a movie. As if this whole thing was happening to someone else. The flock of birds dipped down. The gravestones became clearer and clearer. The birds swooped lower still— and dropped Tavia onto one of the graves. As soon as she was on the ground, the flock scattered, birds of all shapes and sizes disappearing in every direction.

"I'm in the cemetery, lying on a grave," Tavia said aloud, trying to make the situation real. "A bunch of birds brought me here."

And it seemed like the birds had picked out this specific grave. They'd set her down right in front of the tombstone. Except that was ridiculous. Birds didn't have the brains to—

Logic was useless in this situation. Tavia twisted around so she was facing the gravestone. "'Emily Robertson. Beloved Daughter. 1688 to 1703.'"

Let's just say the birds did have the capacity to decide to bring me here, Tavia thought. It's insane, but let's just go with it for a minute. Why? Why here? What does some girl who died three hundred years ago have to do with me?

* * *

The rack. Billy liked the sound of it. The rack. He'd seen one in an old horror movie, seen the guy get stretched and stretched until his skin tore open and his guts popped out. That was what he called punishment. That was what those garbage-eating raccoons deserved.

His rack didn't look like the one in the movie. But Billy figured it would work okay. He stared down at the raccoon. He'd gotten its front paws tied together and anchored to his workbench. Earned himself a nasty bite too, but the little bastard would pay for it.

The raccoon's back feet were tied together with fishing line. Billy figured all he'd have to do was crank the fishing reel. The line would get tight. And Mr. Raccoon would start to stretch.

Billy picked up the reel. It felt good in his hands, cool and solid and heavy. He turned the crank, slowly. He didn't want this to end too fast. Crank, crank, crank. And crank, crank, crank.

The raccoon began to scream. It sounded almost like a woman.

JoJo Johansson stopped off at her best friend Lily's house, the way she did every day on the way to school. They were in the same first grade class and the same Brownie troop. Today they were going to put on a puppet show together. An ecology puppet show. JoJo was going to work the raccoon puppet. Lily was going to work the skunk. They'd made the puppets together in Brownies.

Lily answered the door. "You smell funny," JoJo told her. "Like, I don't know, like burnt butter and onions."

Actually Lily always smelled that way. JoJo had never said anything before because she thought it might hurt Lily's feelings.

And it did. JoJo could see a coating of tears covering Lily's eyeballs. What a baby.

"I don't smell like that," Lily protested.

"Yes you do," JoJo insisted. "And you know what? When you fart, it smells like that too, only worse."

JoJo could tell Lily wanted to say something back. But she couldn't think of anything. Stupid baby. "I don't think I want to be friends with someone who smells as bad as you."

The tears were spilling down Lily's face now. And snot was running out of her nose. Stupid, gross baby.

"You don't want to be my friend?" Lily asked, snuffling as she talked.

"Not really," JoJo answered. "I might consider it, if you give me your special collector's edition Barbie—the wedding one."

"My grandma gave that to me," Lily protested.

"You think anyone else is going to be your friend?" JoJo asked.

Jane stood in the open doorway of her room. She didn't want to go downstairs until her parents had left for work. Looking at either of them just hurt too much. It was as if she could still see the slap marks on their cheeks.

She leaned against the doorframe. She needed a break, a tiny break from what her life had become. "I want to go to when I was little," she whispered to . . . whatever force it was that seemed to control her time slips. She squeezed her eyes shut so tight that the lids ached. "Please."

The texture of the wood beneath her back changed, became rougher. "Prudence, Patience, Hope, and Despair. And a little Hog Island right over there," Jane heard high children's voices chant.

She opened her eyes and found herself in . . . she guessed it was a school. An old-fashioned one-room deal. The littlest children stood in front of the man who must be the teacher.

Older kids sat on rows of benches behind them. A few held books. But most were studying off wooden paddles covered with what looked like thick yellow plastic, although that couldn't be right. Jane could see ABCs and some other stuff—maybe a prayer—written on paper below the plasticy layer.

The last row of benches in the classroom was reserved for the teenage students, the boys separated from the girls. Jane noticed that one of the boys looked like he was about to nod off, his gray eyes drifting closed.

"That rhyme should help you remember the names of the islands around the Colony of Rhode Island," the teacher told the little kids.

"Why isn't Raven's Point in the rhyme?" a little girl with curly black hair asked.

"There are many islands that aren't mentioned," the teacher told her. "Maybe we should try to make up a rhyme for them."

What am I doing here? Jane wondered. She thought she'd be maybe in her canopy bed with her mom reading her a bedtime story. Or playing Candyland with Elijah. It was a pretty dorky thing to have wished for, but it had been what she wanted.

What made me think I could tell It—whatever It is that sends me on these little trips—what to do? Jane asked herself. Yes, it had seemed as if she'd asked a question and gotten an answer a couple times. But this thing, this It, was definitely not under her control. Just hang on and you'll be out of here soon, she thought. At least that's how it had been before.

"Joshua, Michael, Mary-Beth, please come forward," the teacher called. Three of the teenagers moved to the front of the room. Jane couldn't believe how long the girl's hair was. Her auburn braids hung past her waist.

"Mary-Beth, I'd like to hear you recite the passage from Psalms you have memorized," the teacher instructed. "Mary-Beth," he repeated, his voice sharpening, "I expect your full attention."

He definitely didn't have it. Because Mary-Beth was staring at Jane. None of the other kids seemed to see her. But Mary-Beth was staring right at her. The girl's mouth opened, and Jane knew in one more second Mary-Beth was going to scream her head off.

But before she could, the door to the little school opened and a tall man dressed all in black entered. "I need you and all the children to come with me," he told the teacher.

"Certainly, Reverend Abernathy," the teacher answered. "Form a line, please, children. And follow me."

Mary-Beth was still staring at Jane. But one of the

guys—Jane thought it was the one named Joshua—grabbed her by the arm and hauled her into the line ahead of him. The schoolroom quickly emptied. Jane hesitated for a moment, and then followed the students. She was here until It decided she should leave, so why not?

The reverend led the line of kids down the dirt street toward the church. Adults joined the group as they walked. No one talked. No one smiled. It was bizarre. What was with these people? Just because they didn't have flush toilets or television didn't mean they had to walk around like zombies, did it?

When they reached the churchyard, the reverend came to a stop beside a deep, narrow hole. What's that for? Jane wondered. It looked freshly dug, dark-brown earth piled around it.

"My friends, as you know, these have been dark times for the island of Raven's Point," the reverend said, his voice deep and loud and self-important, as if he were taking part in a play or something. "But we have discovered the source of the evil. Our good neighbor, Mr. George Robertson, was possessed by a witch. The witch caused him to take an ax to his own wife. Do not fear, though. For Mr. Robertson has seen the witch's face, and today we, all of us together, with the Lord's help, will put an end to the terror she has brought to our village." The reverend turned toward the church. "Bring forth the witch," he cried.

"Does he honestly believe in the existence of a—" a woman behind Jane began.

"Hush," another woman said harshly. "How dare you question the reverend after what has happened here. My own little girl killed her baby brother. Are you saying that is natural?"

The women fell silent as two men appeared from behind the white church building. A young woman—Jane didn't think she was more than twenty—walked passively between them. Her dark hair hung in her face, but Jane caught a glimpse of her eyes. Make that her eye. She had one brown eye that was whole. But where the other eye should be was an empty socket, red and white with scar tissue.

The men marched the woman over to the hole, gripping her arms tightly, although she didn't struggle. They lifted her up, and placed her inside. One of the men knelt down and held the woman by her shoulders, his fingers digging into her flesh, making Jane's shoulders ache in sympathy. The other man retrieved a shovel and began to fill the hole, trapping the woman inside, with just her head above the ground.

"Each of us, from the youngest to the oldest, must do his share in putting the witch to death," the reverend announced. "Any who does not has clearly already been consumed by the devil and must also be put to death. Our island must be cleansed of evil."

A woman to the left of Jane pulled a large rock out of her apron pocket. Jane's eyes darted around the crowd. They all held rocks now. They were going to stone that woman because they'd decided she was a witch. "No!" Jane shouted. "You're wrong. Leave her alone."

No one heard her. Except the girl from the schoolroom, Mary-Beth. She whipped her head toward Jane, and she started to scream. The man with the shovel stepped up to

Mary-Beth. He pushed a stone into her hand. "Have no fear. God is with us."

"No!" Jane yelled again. The next instant a rock hit the woman in the temple with a wet thunk. Blood began to flow down her face, running into her eye socket, giving her a new eye, an eye of blood.

Jane's knees buckled and she sank down to the carpet. Carpet. Not dirt. Carpet. She ran her fingers over the soft beige pile. She was back.

What was that? Jane thought, still stroking the carpet. Why would It shove me all the way back to colonial days? As if I don't have enough problems right here in the present.

I have kept this puny body alive scores of years
longer than is natural. There is nothing to feed me
here—no jealousy, no anger, no hatred. No fear I
can nurture into something darker. No love that I
can twist into its opposite.

This species lives and dies with only the desire to
find food, to mate, to find food, to mate. Yes, there
are moments of violence, moments of lust. There is
competition. But these animal instincts are weak
and watery and do not nourish me.

Still, I have sucked in what is available. And as the
sun has risen and set over and over I have managed
to grow strong. Stronger. It is time for me to
move closer to the creatures I crave, the creatures
who will feed me until my power is
that of a thousand suns.

The distance from my little flapping, squawking
body to that world is too vast. I must use an
intermediary. I have found the perfect new host. It
will bring me closer. And in one more jump I will
be among my true prey. My prey and my creators.
Humans.

Chapter 7

What the Raven Gave Her

The last bell rang. Screw practice, Seth thought. He had to find out what those ghosts wanted from him. If he didn't, he was sure they'd be back.

The public library was only two blocks away from the high school. Seth didn't bother with his car. He sprinted. There had to be some stuff about Raven's Point's history over there, and reading up on the island was his only chance of getting himself ghost free.

Seth forced himself to a walk a few steps before he reached the library doors. No need to piss Mrs. Sanders off when he was going to need her help. He stepped into the overheated library, pulling in a lungful of the dry air, took off his jacket, and headed over to Mrs. Sanders's desk.

Tavia Burrows got there a second before he did. It's not going to kill you to wait two seconds, he told himself, shifting his weight from one foot to the other.

"I'm interested in finding out about a girl who lived on the island," Tavia told the librarian. "She died in 1703. Were there newspapers then?"

Seth stepped up next to Tavia. "Actually, that's sort of what I was going to ask too. I wanted to know about, like, colonists on Raven's Point."

"It's always nice to see people interested in our island's history," Mrs. Sanders said. "Since you two are such trustworthy individuals, I'll allow you into the rare book room. You won't be able to check out any of the materials, but you're welcome to stay and read as long as you like."

"I didn't even know there was a rare book room," Seth said as they followed Mrs. Sanders down the stairs to the library basement.

"Maybe that's because it's not located on a basketball court," Mrs. Sanders teased. She led the way down the narrow hallway and unlocked the second door on the right. "It's not much of a room, as you'll see. More of a big closet. But it has all the materials on the early history of Raven's Point."

She pointed to a shelf with a row of small boxes. "The newspapers are on microfiche. But you might find the journals even more interesting. I always think it's best to learn history through the words of people who actually lived it." Mrs. Sanders pointed to the top left shelf. "Those up there are from the time period you're interested in."

"Mrs. Sanders, I'm sending one more down to you," a guy called from the top of the basement steps.

"Is there a school assignment about the island history? Should I be expecting hordes?" Mrs. Sanders asked.

Seth exchanged a look with Tavia. She gave a little shrug. "No assignment. Just curious," Seth answered.

"Me too," Tavia said.

"Is this the place where I can find out if there was ever a witch trial or something like that here, back in the olden days?" Jane Romano asked, appearing in the doorway.

Seth smiled. It just happened. He saw her. He smiled. Then she pulled off her hat, a goofy knitted thing, striped, with a pom-pom on top, and her hair came springing out around her face, all that soft light-brown hair. So of course he had to start imagining his fingers in it.

"What?" Jane asked. And Seth realized he was staring like a humongous idiot. "Do I have hat hair?"

"No. It looks great," Seth told Jane. Tavia gave him a knowing smile. What was up with that?

"Well, story hour will be starting up shortly. I'll leave you three to it. Jane, the others can fill you in on the lay of the land," Mrs. Sanders said. "I'm sure I don't have to tell you that there's no eating or drinking down here."

"Thanks," Seth said, Jane and Tavia echoing him. Mrs. Sanders shut the door behind her, leaving them alone.

"I know I'm looking for 1703-ish," Tavia said, staring up at the row of journals.

"I think that's around when my witch hunt thingie was," Jane added, shooting a searching glance at Tavia. "Probably at least seventeen something."

"I'm going for sometime around then too. I'm looking for . . . uh, some kind of disaster or just anything that killed a bunch of people," Seth answered. "Want to tag team it?" he asked quickly before Jane or Tavia could start asking him questions. "We could each take a stack of the journals." He started pulling the old books off the shelf.

"Sounds good to me. I want to know everything about someone named Emily Robertson," Tavia said. She sat down at the small table jammed in the center of the room. Seth handed her a stack of the musty journals, then sneezed into his cupped hand. No Kleenex of course. So now he was standing here in front of Jane with snot on his fingers. Maybe he could wipe his hand on the side of his jeans really fast? Very classy, McFadden, he thought. Then she'd never go out with you. Not that he was planning on asking. There was no reason to start taking advice from Terry Rheingold on girls. It's not like Rheingold had any actual experience either.

"Here." Seth felt something soft against his fingers. He looked down, and Jane pressed a Kleenex—a Kleenex with little smiley faces on it—into his hand.

He blushed. From his neck all the way to his forehead. And it just got worse and worse. "Thanks," he muttered. He cleaned off his hand as fast as he could, then handed Jane a stack of journals and took a bunch for himself. He took the seat next to Tavia. Jane sat down across from him.

"Unless you think something called hog's head cheese could have killed a lot of people, there's nothing in this one," Tavia announced. She held a thin clothbound book. "I did a flip through. It has the cheese recipe and a bunch of other ones, plus cleaning schedules and statistics about how many eggs the hens laid." She put it in the center of the table and picked up the next journal in her stack.

Seth opened the thickest journal in his pile and scanned

the first page, then skipped ahead a few pages, then a bunch of pages more. "Sermons," he told Jane and Tavia. "Long ones. These people must have spent heavy-duty hours in church."

"Does it say who wrote them?" Jane asked, leaning toward them, giving Seth a whiff of tangy lemon perfume. He held himself back from pulling in a deep lungful. "Let's see." He checked the inside cover. "Reverend Bram Abernathy."

"Abernathy?" Jane's voice came out in a squeak. "Can I see that?"

Seth handed over the book. "You heard of him?"

"No," Jane said, eyes on the book. "But I'm looking for stuff on witch trials, and the church and witch trials kind of go together."

Tavia put another journal in the center of the table. "This one's written by a man who lived in Rhode Island, not Raven's Point. It seems like he wrote down every meal he ever ate and every conversation he ever had. Even the ones about the weather."

Seth opened a dark-green journal. *For Maureen Finn on her Nineteenth Birthday*, was written on the first page. His eyes returned to the name—Maureen Finn. It sounded familiar. But why? No one he knew. Someone from the tube? Or a book? His brain itched as he tried to come up with the answer. Maureen Finn. Maureen Finn.

"These sermons get scarier and scarier," Jane said, pulling Seth away from his thoughts.

"Scarier how?" Tavia asked.

"More about the devil walking among them, about how

they all have to arm themselves against evil," Jane answered. "The last one has a bunch of quotes from the Book of Revelations. Lots of end-of-the world stuff. And warnings about them all ending up like the first Raven's Point colonists."

"Is there a date on the last one?" Tavia asked.

Jane flipped back a few pages. "February 10, 1703," she answered. "That's the year you were interested in. You want to look at it?"

"Maybe later," Tavia said.

Seth turned to the next page of Maureen Finn's journal. "This one's from 1701. The girl who kept it worked at a pub owned by a family named Robertson—you said you wanted to know about Emily Robertson, right?" Tavia nodded, leaning over his shoulder so she could see the journal for herself. He flipped ahead a couple pages. "Mostly she's complaining about how little her room is and how hard she has to work." He flipped some more. "Complaining. Complaining."

Suddenly, he felt the little hairs on his neck stand up. "Now she's suddenly talking about second sight." Second sight was like ESP or something. Could the girl who wrote this see ghosts too? Maybe he was onto something with this book.

"Second sight. That could be considered witchcraft," Jane burst out. "It sounds like exactly what I need."

"I want to know anything there is to know about the Robertson family," Tavia added, leaning even closer.

"Read it to us, Seth," Jane urged.

"Okay. Here goes," Seth answered.

November 12, 1702

I went for a stroll along the beach today. I always feel a great deal of contentment when I am able to spend a stretch of Time Alone with Nature. Many days my work at the Pub keeps me occupied from sunup until well after sundown.

I could never complain about my work. Yet, I must say it felt delicious to have the Sun on my face, even the cold Sun of November. Because I was alone, and the fishermen would not return to shore for hours, I made knots in the sides of my skirt to keep the hem above my ankles. I walked as close to the sea spray as I could. I imagined I was a Mermaid with a shining blue and green tail, just as I used to do when I was a girl back in Ireland. Thus immersed in my World of Imagination, did I almost miss the Sign that had been left on the beach. Fortunately, the Pure White Feather caught my eye. I knew at once it was the feather of a Raven. I knew at once as well that the feather was a message.

My granny taught me many things about the World of the Spirits and about Signs and Portents and about the Creatures who may Guide Us. The White Raven is the Special Friend of those with the

Second Sight. Our island was named after the Special Friend, and I have been longing to see the White Raven since I arrived, though I've heard tell the Raven disappeared when the last of the Others took her own life. Oh, I hate to think on that other group of settlers, especially at night before I go to sleep.

I will think about the Feather instead. I do not have this Gift. But sure as I'm writing this, I know the Feather was meant for me. Something Grand is going to happen on our Island. I wish I had the Vision to know if 'twill be Good or Evil. All I do know is 'twill be Grand. It will change all our Lives.

"Keep going," Tavia ordered, her voice hard-edged with impatience.

"It's just more complaining," Seth explained. "She has a cold. Blah, blah." He flipped ahead. "Her hands are raw from washing dishes." He flipped again. "Someone pinched her bottom in the pub. Very rude." He turned to the next page. "Okay, here we go."

November 30, 1702

I fear the White Feather 'twas an Omen of bad things to come. I can only pray 'twill not be as bad as what happened to the Others, the ones who came first. When the Evil appeared to me, 'twas near time for the Pub to close. I gathered up a load of scraps for the cobbler's dog, who had been waiting so patiently outside the back door. I have always had a Fondness for that dog. He's a beautiful thing, is Shep, with hair of black and silver. He and I, we've been Friends since he was a pup.

Tonight it was as if he had never Laid Eyes on me. I threw the scraps down at his feet. He did not give them a look, nor even a sniff. No, he Bared his Teeth, curling his lip back something awful. Then he moved toward me. His belly 'most touched the ground he kept himself so low.

"What Ails you, Shep?" I asked him. The creature growled at me in reply. My Heart gave a shiver in my chest. Then he Leapt at me. Before I could make a sound, his teeth scraped across my eye. And I swear it on My Life, he grinned at me. I swear that I saw it as the blood was flowing from my eye.

"Oh, my god," Jane whispered. "That's horrible."

"But why'd she say 'the evil' appeared to her?" Tavia asked. "It was just a dog."

"I don't even want to think about what happened to those 'others' she keeps talking about," Jane added.

"Well, this Maureen chick is a little dramatic," Seth reminded them. But his head was filled with the image of the dog smiling, smiling as Maureen's warm blood ran down its throat.

"Go on. What happens next?" Jane asked. "Don't skip anything."

Obediently, Seth began to read.

December 2, 1702

I now spend my days in the kitchen of the Pub. I have washed so many dishes and peeled so many potatoes that my hands have the appearance of Raw Meat. I do not like to complain, not after all the Kindness that has been shown to me, but I do so miss the Companionship and Society of being in the front of the Pub. Trotting back and forth with the food and drink, I heard every scrap of news about our village. And there was always someone to give me a friendly wink or a smile.

Mr. Robertson says my Injury is disturbing to look at. He says the men do not like to gaze on my Eye while they sup, the place where my Eye used to be, I mean to say. I still feel it there, though the doctor had to remove it due to Infection. So I stay in the back and Earn my Keep. I have yet to even repay Mr. Robertson for my Passage, let alone my food and bed. I am sorry that my Injury, the Wound the Horrible Beast inflicted on me, has made me less valuable to my sponsor.

I did hear a scrap of gossip. It's said that today is the anniversary of the first atrocity. I do not know how Mr. Baily can know this, but he says that on this day, seven years ago, the first of the Others committed the darkest sin I think I've ever heard of. This is the day one of the others killed his child and fed off it to save his own life. What a horrible history my new home has. Why did I ever come here?

December 25, 1702

Today we celebrate the birth of Our Lord Jesus Christ. It should be such a happy day, but no one on our Island is happy. Grief and Misfortune have struck almost everyone. Some have had small injuries, such as Mrs. Peterson and her scalded hand. Some have had Great Calamities—like the capsizing of Mr. Hadley's boat. Most of the crew was Lost that day.

The Worst of it is that many in the Village have begun to blame me for Our Unhappy Times. It is my empty Eye, I know that. It frightens them. Some think 'tis a Sign that I have attracted the attention of a demon. Some fear it is the same

demon that took hold of the first colonists. For no
humans could have behaved as they did without the
interference of the Dark Forces.

The Robertsons have remained True to me. I
continue to work for them. But now I live alone in
a small hut at the far end of the pasture. Mr.
Robertson said he wanted me to be close to the sheep
in case one is injured or becomes ill. But I know he
lies. I have been Banished because even Mr.
Robertson has come to Fear me a little.

"Sounds like you might have found your disaster, Seth," Jane said.

"Or disasters," Tavia added. "Am I wrong, or did the first Raven's Point colonists—"

"Have a Donner Party party," Seth finished for her, trying to keep his tone light even though bile was forcing its way up his throat.

Tavia nodded.

"It sure sounds like it," Seth answered.

"Except the people in the Donner Party ate their dead," Jane commented, face pale. "They didn't kill to stay alive."

Seth didn't have anything to say to that. Neither did Tavia. They sat in silence for a moment, and Seth started thinking about the shipwreck. Those men with the seaweed in their hair—could they be the ghosts of the crew of Mr. Hadley's boat?

How surreal was it that he was actually asking himself

that question? But either he was seeing ghosts or he was totally psychotic. And he was rooting against psychotic.

"Read some more," Tavia said. "I want to see if she ever talks about Emily Robertson."

Seth cleared his throat, wishing for a 7UP, and began to read again.

January 14, 1703

A Strange and Horrible event befell me today. I was huddled close to the hearth, trying to stay warm, when I heard a Thumping on my door. I rushed over to open it, so excited was I at the thought of having Company. It has been too long since I have seen a Human face. Imagine my surprise when I opened the door to find a Raven standing there, a Raven white as Snow.

With two mighty flaps of its wings, it was on my shoulder. And then 'twas a kind of Miracle, because inside the empty hole where my eye used to be, a Vision formed. I was given the Gift of the Second Sight. Or perhaps it would be more true to call it a Curse. But the Raven brought it to me, of that I am sure.

The vision, oh, 'tis almost too horrible to write down. But I saw young Jack Mason rowing over to the little island where the Masons keep their goats. I saw young Jack make a Noose. And then I saw him string up goat after goat. I do not know how a boy so Small had the strength, but hang the goats he did, more than a dozen from the branches of the oak trees on the Island.

I pondered over what to do with my Vision. Then I decided it was my Responsibility to try and stop the Awful Deed. So I went to my Sponsor, my Kind Mr. Robertson. He told me to Hush. He told me never to speak of the Visions again. He told me to return to my Hut and stay there if I wanted to continue to have his Care and Support.

Perhaps my Vision was untrue. I Pray that it was. I Pray that I slept and dreamed of the White Raven and the Change it brought about in me. But Deep in my Heart, I know that everything I saw will come to Be.

Christ. The boy with the noose. Seth had seen his ghost too. He didn't wait for Tavia or Jane to tell him to go on. He sucked in some air and kept reading.

February 2, 1703

What an awful day this one has been. My Kind Mr. Robertson came bursting into my hut without even a knock. He grabbed me by my shoulders and shook me hard. "How did you know about the goats?" he demanded.

And I knew my Vision had come to Be. The Goats had been hung in the trees of their little Island. I tried to explain about the White Raven and the Second Sight, but Mr. Robertson clamped his hand over my mouth. He told me to Hush. He told me never, ever to speak of my Visions again. He had taken me in. He had given his Support to me. Everything I did reflected on him, he said. And if Anyone heard that I Knew of the Slaughter before it happened, his business could be Ruined. As for me, he didn't like to think of what might happen to me if 'twere Revealed that I Saw it all before it happened. Of course, I agreed to stay Silent.

"So, what do we think?" Tavia asked. "Was she delusional? Did anyone around her even know this stuff was brewing in her head?"

Seth pictured the ghosts—the drowned men, the boy with the noose. Maureen's telling the truth, he thought. But he kept his mouth shut. He didn't want Tavia and Jane to start wondering if *he* was delusional.

"I don't know," Jane answered. "I mean, people can have premonitions, can't they? Just because you have a vision doesn't mean you're crazy, right?"

Tavia sighed. "Who's to say what crazy is?"

"Not me," Seth replied. He returned to the journal.

March 13, 1703

I have grown used to having only the sheep for company. I have named them all, and I often walk among them, telling them the stories my granny used to tell me, happy stories of Elves and Leprechauns.

I can tell you I was not happy when I heard the flapping of huge Wings. I yelled at the Raven to fly away when it landed on my shoulder. But it clung on tight, its Talons digging into my skin, leaving small red holes.

Of course, the White Raven brought me a Vision. A Vision of Mr. Robertson cutting off his Wife's head with his Ax. Who can I tell? No one. But the Vision will come to be, by and by. I know that. But what can I do except Tend to my Sheep. And pray.

Seth went right on to the next entry without pausing.

March 21, 1703

The White Raven visits me daily now. My Shoulder is raw from the grip of its Talons. My head is raw from the horror of the Visions. Such Hideous Occurrences will befall the People of Raven's Point. It is as if all the citizens are to become Gripped by Madness or taken over by the Devil Himself.

I myself will not be Spared. I have seen my own Death. I cannot write of it. My hand will not leave off shaking when I think on it. And yet, Terrifying as it will be, perhaps it will be better to Die than to be Alive for what will come after.

"She's right about her hand shaking," Seth commented. "I could hardly make out the last paragraph."

"What could she possibly have thought was going to happen?" Tavia asked. "What could make her think death might be the best option?"

Jane's eyes darkened. "I can think of a few things I wouldn't want to live to see." She pushed her hands away from her face with both hands. "Let's hear the rest."

Seth studied Jane for a long moment, wondering what she'd been thinking about. He decided not to ask. He continued to read.

April 4, 1703

Mrs. Robertson is Dead. Hacked to bits with an Ax. With her Death my own draws nearer.

But the Raven has given me a Vision of Hope. There is a Way to Stop the Evil that has taken over our Sweet Village. It will take great Courage. The Pain will be almost unbearable. But if the four will do their Duty, the Village will Survive and even Prosper. For a Time.

Tonight I must Creep into the Village and find Joshua. He is younger than I by almost five years. But the Raven has shown me that it is he I must Tell. Whether he will Act on what I Reveal, I cannot say, I have not seen. Still, I must tell him how to Fight the Evil, he and the other three. It will be up to them to Accept their Fate. It is not a choice I can make for them.

Seth was really wishing for that 7UP now. Every drop of his saliva had dried up. His mouth and throat and tongue felt like they were made of sandpaper.

This was it. This was the answer. His ghosts—they were all people who had died, died or done the killing Maureen was describing.

Maureen talked about evil as if it had a life of its own. But that wasn't possible. Seth scrubbed his face with both hands. As if he knew the difference between possible and impossible anymore.

"Don't stop now, Seth. We need to hear it all." Jane's voice came out scratchy, like she might have sandpaper coating her mouth too.

He nodded and began to read.

April 7, 1703

They come for me. I can hear the bootfalls. I can hear their angry voices. It is as the Raven showed me. It is time for me to Die.

The only Hope for the rest is that Joshua Believed me. And that he will be able to Persuade the other three that they must make the Sacrifice.

Seth flipped to the next page. Blank.

"Wait. That's it?" Tavia exclaimed, her voice sharp. "Nothing about Emily Robertson?"

"Nope. That's where it ends," Seth answered, flipping through the journal again to make sure.

"I think the girl who wrote the journal must have been the witch I . . . heard about," Jane said. "I think right after this they came and dragged her to the church and stoned her."

"Heard it where?" Tavia asked.

"Just . . . around," Jane said, neatening up the stack of journals in front of her. "A Halloween story maybe."

"Would have been nice if Maureen had actually written

down the way to stop the evil," Seth said.

"Yeah," Jane and Tavia answered together.

Suddenly Jane gave a choked laugh.

"What could you possibly find funny right now?" Tavia asked.

"I was just thinking about the tourists," Jane answered. "You know how they get fed the story about how the island was named for a white raven that is still supposed to be alive today."

"And anyone who sees it is supposed to have good luck for the rest of their lives," Tavia finished for her. She raised her eyebrows. "Didn't work too well for our Maureen did it?"

"Just think if the real story came out," Jane continued. "McGrady's Grocery would never sell another white raven pendant, that's for sure."

"But the raven told Maureen how to save the rest of the people on the island. Assuming she wasn't a complete whack job, that is," Seth said. "I guess that's a twisted kind of good luck."

Jane's face grew serious again. "I wonder if it worked," she said softly.

If it hadn't worked, maybe that's why his ghosts were still around. Maybe that's what they'd left unfinished.

But why in the hell would they be expecting me to fix it for them? Can't they look at me and see that there's no way I could handle something like that?

Chapter 8

Such Hideous Occurrences

Thomas emptied another jug of bleach into the bathtub, the fumes searing his lungs. He ignored the pain. He twisted open the top on the next jug. *Glug, glug, glug.* The jug emptied into the tub.

He studied the tub full of bleach with satisfaction. She wants a white boy? Not a problem. Thomas shucked off his clothes, stepped into the tub, and lay down. The bleach came up to his chin. His skin started to itch immediately. Then to burn. Good. That meant it was working. He dunked a washcloth in the bleach and began to scrub his face. Itching. Then burning. Good.

The new lights on the driveway basketball court were off. At least something was going his way. Seth stepped into the house and immediately knew it was empty. Even better. He wasn't in the mood to put on the I'm-not-going-to-screw-up-again show for his parents.

He wandered into the kitchen, grabbed the two-liter 7UP out of the fridge, and started chugging it. Slowly the sandpaper in his throat dissolved. Seth stuck the bottle back in the fridge noticing the note from his mom. "Your dad and I are at bridge, remember? Order pizza." A twenty-dollar bill was stuck under the plastic strawberry magnet above the note.

It just gets better and better, Seth thought, promising himself that he'd order a small even though he had enough cash for one of those giant New York–style deals.

"Oh, Mom," he said aloud when he saw that she'd left the phone book open with the number for the one pizza place that delivered off-season circled in red. He'd be leaving for college next year and she still wasn't sure he could use the phone book by himself. He grabbed the phone and started to press the buttons for the circled number. Three numbers in, it registered that the number belonged to the Romano's, not Pizza Town.

"Just trying to help you out, buddy."

Seth turned around. "If you really want to help me out, tell me how someone like me is supposed to stop some creeping evil and put a bunch of ghosts to rest."

"I'm more interested in getting you laid, weenie," Terry answered.

And he was gone.

"Thanks a lot," Seth muttered. He started to slam the phone book shut, then hesitated.

Who were you, Emily Robertson? Tavia thought as she pulled into her driveway. She'd searched every journal after

Seth had finished reading, but there was no other mention of anyone in the Robertson family. The microfiche was no help. The paper stopped coming out about six months before Emily died. When it started back up again, more than four months later, all the news was ordinary—weddings and weather, fishing news and picnics.

Exactly what happened in Raven's Point during the months the paper stopped coming out? Tavia wondered. Exactly how had Emily died? She turned off the engine, unfastened her seat belt, and climbed out of the car. There couldn't have really been some supernatural force or the dev—

Her eyes brushed over the front lawn. Something was out there. Lying on the ground. Tavia couldn't make out details in the dark. But there was definitely something there. Something big.

Maybe I should go get Mom and Dad, Tavia thought as she slammed the car door. But the thing on the lawn, it drew her. Slowly, she approached it. The figure became more clear. Human. She took another step—and it felt as if all the blood drained out of her body, leaving her cold and weak.

"Thomas," she whispered. It's not him, she thought. It can't be him.

She took one more step. And she could no longer pretend it wasn't Thomas lying there. "What happened to you? Oh, god. Thomas." She knelt beside him. He was still, so still. And his skin . . . So raw. In places it had been . . . it looked like it had been scraped completely off. She could see muscle. And . . . was that? Yes, she could see a piece of his cheekbone.

Was he dead? Could he be alive and look like that?

"Thomas!" Tavia cried. "Thomas!" She knelt down beside him, eyes locked on his chest. Was it moving? She reached out to shake him. But there was nowhere to touch. Every inch of skin she could see was . . . wounded.

"I'll get help," she promised him. "I'll be right back, Thomas."

His eyes opened. They were bloodshot and swollen, but they locked onto Tavia with an intensity that squeezed the breath from her lungs. "I did it for you, Eight," he croaked.

Tavia shoved herself to her feet and bolted up the porch steps. "I'll get help," she yelled, not looking back. She flew into the house. "Mom! Dad!" she screeched.

Her father was at her side almost instantly. "What? What's wrong?"

"It's Thomas," Tavia burst out. "He's . . . I don't know. I don't know."

"Take a breath, honey," her mother said as she came up behind Tavia's father.

Obediently, Tavia sucked in a breath. It didn't help much. But a little. "Thomas is on the front lawn. Maybe he passed out there. I don't—"

Her dad took her by the shoulders and moved her out of his way, then he slammed out the front door. "Come sit down," her mother urged.

Tavia shook her head. She had to get back out there. "Call an ambulance, Mom." Her mother opened her mouth to speak. "I'm okay. Please, just call." Then Tavia forced herself to walk back out of the house and over to Thomas's side.

Help him, help him, somebody help him, Tavia silently

prayed. A cat slunk out from under the hydrangea bush and wound itself around Tavia's legs, mewing pitifully.

"I'm afraid to touch him," her father said. "I'm afraid his skin would just come off in my hands. What in the hell happened to him?"

The cat gave another long mew. A dog gave a wail in the distance, a chorus of low howls joining in. "Nothing you guys can do, I know," Tavia said softly. "Mom's getting an ambulance," she told her father. She knelt next to Thomas again. His eyes were closed. And she was glad they were.

"What's that smell?" her father asked. He crouched down next to Tavia and put his arm around her shoulders. The cat stayed pressed close against her side.

Tavia hadn't noticed the smell. The horror of Thomas's mutilated body had consumed her. But there was a smell. Harsh and clean. And ordinary. "I think it's bleach."

"Yeah, you're right," her dad answered. "Enough bleach would do it all right."

You want to be with somebody white. Your mother got herself a white man, why shouldn't you? That's it, isn't it?

The words exploded through Tavia's head in Thomas's voice. Whiteness. Bleach.

I did it for you, Eight.

Tavia leapt to her feet and turned away from Thomas. She couldn't look at him. He'd done that to himself. She knew it. Done it to himself for her. She wrapped her arms tightly around her body. She didn't turn around when she heard the wail of the ambulance. Or when she heard the EMTs gather around Thomas. She closed her eyes and lowered her head, and didn't move. Her mother came outside and pulled her close. The cat gently head butted her leg. But it didn't help. Tavia could hardly feel. It was as if her mother and the cat were ghosts, unable to really touch her.

Matthew poked a small hole in the top of one of his dad's beers and poured out some of the brew, maybe a quarter of a can. Then he used an eyedropper with an extra thin tube—he'd lifted it from chem lab—to replace the missing beer with Liquid Plumr. It took forever, but Matthew went ahead and doctored half the cans in the twelve-pack.

"Your choice, Dad," Matthew whispered. "If you decide to get off your fat ass, leave your beers behind, and actually do something—like challenge me to a game of horse—then you'll be fine. Otherwise, tonight you'll be playing another kind of game—Russian roulette."

"Dum, dum, da dum," JoJo hummed to herself as she marched her brand-new Special Edition Barbie down a church aisle made of a long strip of pink toilet paper. "Your wedding dress is beautiful," she told Barbie. "But you need bridesmaids."

JoJo tilted her head to the side. Yeah, the Special Edition Olsen Twin Barbies Lily had would be perfect as bridesmaids. Twin bridesmaids—nothing was cooler than that. And Lily would definitely give them to her. Maybe JoJo would have to tell some kids at school that Lily always wore diaper things to slumber parties because she still wet the bed. If she did that, then no one would want to be friends with stupid, gross, baby Lily. Lily would be so glad JoJo still even talked to her that she'd hand over the Olsen Twin Barbies like that.

Jane stared at herself in the full-length mirror attached to the inside of her closet door. Too dressy? Not dressy enough? Trying way too hard? She knew the answer to that one. She was definitely trying way too hard. But did it look like she was trying way too hard? Or was it okay to look like you were trying at least somewhat hard? Wouldn't a guy be happy to know that you put in some effort before you went out with him?

She was going out with Seth McFadden. She still couldn't believe it. The night after they'd run into each other he'd called her up, and, bam, asked her if she wanted to go to the dance; and two days later, here she was getting ready. Seth had sounded almost as surprised to be asking as she had been to be asked.

Jane checked the clock. She still had enough time to change. She frowned at her jean skirt and peasant blouse. Too trendy? It was the combo of the moment. But did guys know that? And was it bad to wear the thing that was in all the magazines?

A knock at her door pulled Jane away from her thoughts. "Can I come in?" her mother called.

"Sure," Jane answered.

Her door swung open. "Oh, you look so sweet," Jane's mom exclaimed.

Sweet. Huh, Jane thought. Not exactly what I was going for.

"Are you excited?" her mother asked.

Jane couldn't stop a big stupid grin from spreading across her face. "Kinda," she admitted.

"Kinda," her mom said back, imitating Jane. "Back when I used to go on dates I was usually more than kinda excited."

"Where'd you and Dad go on your first date?" Jane blurted out. She knew the answer. But she wanted to hear her mother talk about her father with that gushy sound in her voice.

"We went bowling. Which I know sounds old-fashioned and boring, but with your dad it was so—" Jane's mother stopped abruptly.

"So what?" Jane prompted.

Jane's mom gave her head a tiny shake. I'm an idiot, Jane thought. I made her all sad. Why wouldn't thinking about how she and Dad were back then make her sad when now they can't even stand to be in the same room? "Thanks for buying me the new boots and everything," Jane said, trying to change the subject.

The doorbell rang. "That's gotta be him," Jane said, sounding freaked.

"Oh, no. The cute basketball player is here. Everybody run!" her mother teased. She brushed Jane's light-brown hair away from her face. "You look beautiful."

Beautiful. That was much better than sweet, Jane thought. But it *was* her mother talking.

"Do you want me to answer?" her mother asked.

"No, it's okay, I got it," Jane said quickly. At least she didn't have to worry about any Elijah weirdness. Or any parent slap fights. Her dad had taken Elijah for a drive.

Jane grabbed a breath freshener strip out of the little pack on her dresser and stuck it in her mouth. It would be gone by the time she reached the bottom of the stairs. And her breath would be minty fresh. For Seth. Seth. She was going out with Seth.

"You sure you don't want me to answer it?" her mother asked.

Jane realized she was still standing in her bedroom. "I'm sure. Bye, mom!" She raced out of her room and down the hall, then forced herself to slow down and take the stairs one at a time. Her new boots had higher heels than she was used to. She didn't want to break her neck before she even left the house. She also didn't want to sound like a herd of elephants tromping down the stairs. Not the impression she was going for.

"Hi," Jane said as she swung open the door. "You ready to go? I'm ready." I also sound like an idiot, she thought. She turned away from Seth to grab her coat off the coat tree. She jammed her arm in one sleeve, then tried for the other sleeve. And missed. God, I'm looking like such a klutz, she thought. She made another stab at the sleeve. And there it was. In perfect position. She slid her arm in easily, and realized Seth was holding it for her. He was helping her on with her coat. "Thanks," she said, looking up into his blue eyes. She realized this was the first moment she'd looked directly at his face. She'd given her hello speech talking to his chest. Lame.

"You look great," Seth told her. "But I'm kinda missing the hat with the pom-pom."

Jane felt herself blushing. She so did not want to be

blushing. "That's more of a daytime hat," she answered. Was everything that came out of her mouth tonight going to sound stupid?

"So you said you were ready to go?" Seth said.

"Right. Yes. I am. Let's do that," Jane answered. Seth moved to the side so Jane could go out first. She locked the door behind them and they headed to Seth's car. I should know what kind of car it is, Jane thought. Then I could say nice whatever kind of car. And it was a nice car. Most people on the island drove rust buckets because the salt air eventually corroded everything anyway. Seth's was actually a mainland kind of car.

Seth opened the door for her and Jane slid inside. A car really is like its own little world, Jane thought as Seth slid behind the wheel. Right now we're on planet Jane/Seth. Jeethsan.

"What are you smiling about?" Seth asked as he pulled out onto the street.

Jane felt herself blush. Again. "I was just thinking if the two of us created like a new planet it could be called Jeethsan." Now that was beyond idiotic. A lie, Jane. Ever heard of one? she asked herself. They can be useful for not humiliating yourself.

"That or San-Jeeth. That sounds sort of *Star Wars*-ish," Seth answered, as though Jane had said something totally normal.

Jane laughed. "Greetings. I represent the planet San-Jeeth to the Jedi council."

Seth laughed too. It was like his laugh had a physical presence, like big warm bubbles popping against her face.

"So, I don't think I've seen you at any of the school dances before," Seth said.

All the laughter drained out of Jane's body. That means he's noticed what a loser I am, she thought. She actually had gone to dances, spent the night hanging out in a tight little cluster of girl friends who were also not getting asked to dance. But somehow after the accident, she'd just started staying home more. She made it to basketball games—because she needed those few hours of Seth watching to survive—but that was about it. It felt like her parents needed her around, needed to see her walking around coma free. Months passed, months and months, and somehow, everyone else had moved on ahead.

"I used to—" Jane started again. "I've gone to a few. Those things are so crowded you never see everybody."

Seth nodded as he pulled into the school parking lot. We're here already, Jane realized. In a place as small as Raven's Point, you never had far to drive.

"I usually go, hang out with the guys on the team who aren't going out with anyone," Seth told her.

"I know the type. Standing by the bleachers, acting all superior," Jane teased. She'd just made fun of Seth McFadden.

Seth laughed, that laugh that made her feel like she was laughing too, even though she wasn't. "That's me. But it's not superiority. It's fear of dancing." He parked the car, got out. Jane already had her door half open before she realized he'd trotted around the car to open it for her.

"Thanks," she said. And then she found herself walking toward the gym with Seth McFadden. He was different than he seemed from a distance. Not that he hadn't seemed like a nice guy when she'd seen him in the hallways or in the caf or on the court. But he hadn't seemed like a goofball who'd make up sci-fi planet names. Or a guy who'd admit to fear of, well, anything. He seemed as if he'd be a guy who could do everything easily. Jane was kind of glad he wasn't. The perfect and the imperfect should never try to go out together.

Seth handed money to Mr. Hennessey, the English teacher. He did not look happy to have pulled dance guard duty. Jane had this wild impulse to reach up and use her fingers to push his mouth into a smile. This could possibly be the most amazing night of her life. Everybody should be happy! Everybody on Raven's Point Island!

"I'll stow our coats," Seth said. He stood behind Jane and slid her coat off her shoulders after she'd unbuttoned it. The slow slide of the coat's silk lining against her thin blouse made her shiver. In a good way. "Be right back," Seth told her.

Jane got that deer-in-the-headlights feeling. What was she supposed to do? Where was she supposed to stand? What kind of expression did she have on her face right now?

Get a grip, she told herself. You know every single person in the place. Go and talk to somebody. But who? Jane had friends, but they were more study-with friends, eat-lunch-with friends. It used to be different. A long time ago.

I'll get us something to drink, Jane decided. She felt better now that she had a purpose. She walked over to the refreshment table and bought two 7UPs. When she turned around with them, there Seth was.

"For me?" Seth said, with exaggerated astonishment.

"For you." Jane handed him one of the 7UPs. They moved away from the refreshment table crowd to drink them.

"Vince's cousin's band is actually starting to sound better," Seth commented, moving closer to her so he could be heard over the drum solo.

"Yeah," Jane agreed, even though she'd only heard The Creators play once before. She'd agree to pretty much anything to keep on standing here, so close to Seth she could feel the heat of his body even though they weren't actually touching. The drummer went into a frenzy of playing, then the gym went silent. Jane clapped her free hand against her 7UP can.

A few moments later, the band started up again, something slow and sort of . . . weepy. One of Vince's cousin's compositions, Jane figured, since she'd never heard the song before.

"So, do you want to dance?" Seth asked.

"I thought you had some dance phobia," Jane replied. You could have just said yes, she scolded herself.

"Not as much of slow dancing." Seth plucked the 7UP out of Jane's fingers and put both their cans on an empty bleacher rung. Then he held out his hand. Please don't let me wake up now, Jane thought as she took it.

But this couldn't be a dream. Even in a dream she wouldn't have been able to come up with this feeling. She had her cheek pressed against Seth's chest and she could feel his heart beating against her skin. His hands were around her waist and hers were looped behind his neck, his silky black hair soft against her fingers. They hardly moved, just swayed back and forth. And instead of being on a planet of their own, like it had been in the car, it was almost like they were sharing a body.

Too soon, much, much too soon, it was over. And he was stepping away, their body ripping into two. At least he didn't let go of her hand. She needed that connection. It would have been too much to go from everything to nothing in one second.

"A fast one," Seth said as the band started up again. "Want to risk it?"

"You want to go get our drinks instead?" Jane asked, smiling at the relief on Seth's face.

"Sure. Great." He led the way over to the bleachers, not letting go of her hand.

"Hey, guys," Lucy Choi called. She headed right over to Seth, took his soda out of his hand, and sucked down a long swallow. "Having fun?" she asked as she handed the 7UP back.

"Yes," Jane answered, even though Lucy'd been looking directly at Seth when she asked the question.

Lucy turned her attention to Jane. "I was just about to go to the ladies' room. You want to come with? Do a little makeup repair?"

"Uh, I guess," Jane answered. If there was mascara all over her face or something, she should deal with it.

"Come on, then." Lucy pulled Jane's hand free of Seth's and towed her toward the ladies' room.

"Be right back," Jane called over her shoulder to Seth.

"I'll be here," he answered.

Lucy picked up speed. When they reached the bathroom, she practically pushed Jane inside. "Very nice, Jane. That's your name, right? Jane?"

"Jane, right," Jane said, trying to figure out what Lucy was so pissed off about.

"Andrea couldn't come tonight because her *mother* is in the *hospital*," Lucy spat out.

"And?" Jane asked. She walked over to the mirrors, just to put some space between her and Lucy. There was nothing wrong with her makeup that she could see, but she pulled out a lipstick. She'd put on a fresh coat and then she was out of here.

"Don't act all innocent." Lucy followed Jane over to the mirrors. "Everyone knows Andrea and Seth have a thing."

Jane flashed on Andrea and Seth standing close together in the hallway. God, Andrea was so gorgeous. Why had Jane even thought— Stop it, she ordered herself. He asked you here. "He asked me here," she said aloud.

"As some kind of weak-ass substitute," Lucy shot back. "Because no girl with any class would say yes when they know what Andrea's going through."

Madeline Gunderson and Elizabeth Reynolds sauntered into the bathroom. "Come over here a minute, you two," Lucy called. "Help me figure out what Seth McFadden could possibly see in this girl, even just for one night." Madeline came up on Jane's left, Elizabeth on her right. Lucy stood almost directly behind Jane.

Jane touched up her lipstick, managing not to end up with clown mouth. Then she returned her lipstick to her purse. Just go, she told herself. What are they going to do, wrestle you to the ground? I don't think so. She turned around and took a step toward the door. Lucy blocked her.

"It's definitely not the hair," Lucy said. She reached out and gave a piece of Jane's hair a hard pull. "It's that ugly dishwater no-color color."

"Not the face," Madeline chimed in. "Look at the eyebrows. Haven't you ever heard of a tweezer?"

"And her eyes are too close together," Elizabeth added.

Lucy reached out and jerked loose the tie at the top of Jane's peasant blouse. She held out the material and peered down at Jane's body. Goose bumps broke out over Jane's exposed flesh. They really aren't going to let me out of here, she thought. They were moving in even tighter, like a pack of dogs going in for the kill.

"Not the breasts, that's for sure," Lucy said to the other girls. "It's the easy factor. That's all I can think of." She returned her attention to Jane. "That's it, right, Jane? You'll spread 'em anytime, anyplace. Maybe we should invite all the guys in here. You'd like that, wouldn't you?"

Think, Jane ordered herself. This is no time to panic. You need to think.

"Andrea must be pretty insecure," she managed to say in a bored-sounding voice. "Is she that afraid that one night with me is going to make Seth forget every other girl in school?"

"Of course not," Lucy snapped. "You're not competition for Andrea."

"Even if I spread 'em?" Jane countered, forcing out the crude words.

"You're not that good," Elizabeth told her.

Jane slowly retied the top of her blouse. "So you don't mind if I go on back out there and dance with Seth? That won't hurt Andrea's chances any?"

Lucy opened the bathroom door. "A night with you will make Seth want Andrea even more."

Jane wanted to sprint out of the bathroom. All she wanted to do was get back over to Seth, back to their own private world. But she forced herself to walk over to the row of mirrors. Let Lucy keep holding the door, she thought as she pulled out her lipstick.

Tavia didn't bother to stop at the gift shop. She knew there was absolutely nothing in there that would be appropriate to give Thomas. But she had to see him. Stairs or elevator? she debated. The *ding* of the elevator made the decision for her. She moved toward the door, and when it opened, she found herself face-to-face with Andrea Callison.

"Andrea, hi," Tavia said. The girl looked like death— pale, her hair greasy and uncombed. "Uh, what are you doing here?" Tavia wasn't sure if she should have asked or not. Clearly there was something very wrong, but Andrea might not want to go there.

"Visiting my mom," Andrea answered. She gave a harsh, barking laugh. "You won't believe this, but she managed to cut off her entire hand. And that's after she sliced off her finger. At least it was the finger of the hand that's now missing."

"How's she doing?" Tavia asked.

"Fine, I guess. I mean, she'll have to have one of those

fake hands and everything," Andrea told her. "But . . . I don't know."

Ask or don't ask? Tavia thought. It seemed like Andrea wanted to keep talking. "Don't know what?"

"The finger, it could have been an accident, okay," Andrea said. She used both hands to scrub her face, and Tavia realized Andrea wasn't wearing any makeup. She didn't think she'd ever seen Andrea's bare face before. "But the hand," Andrea went on, "it pretty much had to be intentional. She went into some supply closet and got a saw thing they use to cut bone in surgery. My mom's not even a surgical nurse. There was no reason for her to touch it. Nobody here has been able to even feed me a decent lie about how it could have accidentally happened."

Tavia felt as if a cold finger had just traced its way down her spine. Like Thomas, she thought. Mrs. Callison attacked herself, just like Thomas. "Had she been acting strange lately?"

Andrea's mouth tightened. "Want all the gossip, Tavia? Want to go back to school with the scoop?"

"No, I—" Tavia began to protest.

"I have to get home." Andrea rushed away without a backward glance. Tavia turned back to the elevator and pushed the Up button. The elevator door opened immediately.

"I'm in no rush," Tavia muttered as she stepped inside and pushed the button for the third floor. She knew exactly where to go when she got off. Thomas's room was in the same place as Elijah's had been, just on a different level. Was this going to be the pattern for the rest of her life? Get close to a guy—visit him in the hospital. Lather, rinse, and repeat.

She took a left and headed down the corridor. Mr. Bledsoe was sitting outside Thomas's room. "Tavia, thank god you're here," he exclaimed. "Nothing will make Thomas feel better than a visit from you." I left out a step, Tavia thought. Get close to a guy, visit him in the hospital, disappoint his grieving father.

Tavia forced a smile at Thomas's father. Clearly he didn't know she and Thomas weren't together. This definitely wasn't the time to tell him. "Is he awake?" she asked.

"In and out," Mr. Bledsoe answered. "His mother's in there with him right now."

Tavia sat down on the plastic chair next to him, a rush of déjà vu hitting her like a wave. How many times had she sat outside Elijah's room with Mr. Romano, back when he thought she was the best girl in the world, his true ally. "What have the doctors said?"

Mr. Bledsoe shook his head. "Second degree burns over his entire body. A few third degree in areas where the skin is especially sensitive."

Tavia winced, sympathy pains shooting through her like electric shocks. "We just don't understand why he would do such a thing," Mr. Bledsoe continued. "What do you think? Has it seemed as if something was . . . troubling him? The doctors didn't find any drugs in his system, but—"

"Thomas didn't use drugs," Tavia interrupted. Although she guessed in a way that made it worse for Thomas's father. If Thomas used drugs, then he was out of his head when he tried to burn the skin off his body. That made a horrible kind of sense. But knowing Thomas had made a clearheaded decision, that had to be driving Mr. Bledsoe insane.

"I'm going to go get Thomas's mother out of there," Mr. Bledsoe said.

"No, don't," Tavia protested. "I can wait. It's no problem."

"She's been in there too long. She needs a break, whether she wants one or not," he answered. "I'll take her to the cafeteria while you sit with Thomas."

He stood up and hurried into Thomas's hospital room. Tavia stood up too. She smoothed her hands over her head, making sure all her braids were still in place in her ponytail. Yeah, I have to make sure I look good for Thomas, she told herself, since he did this for me. The thought made her feel as if she'd been drinking the same bleach Thomas had used on his skin. She felt raw inside.

Mr. Bledsoe walked Thomas's mom out of the room. She managed to give Tavia a trembling smile. Tavia smiled back, feeling like such a fraud. When Thomas's parents were out of sight, Tavia stepped into Thomas's hospital room. She couldn't see much of him—thank god a sheet was tented over most of his body—but what she could see was swathed in bandages. Thomas's eyes were closed. Tavia couldn't help but feel relieved as she sat down in the chair next to the bed. It was still warm from Mrs. Bledsoe's body.

"Thomas, hi," she said softly, unsure whether he was awake or asleep. "It's me, Tavia." Thomas didn't open his eyes, but Tavia decided to keep going anyway. "I should have come before now. I can't believe it's already been almost two days since . . . Anyway, I've been thinking a lot about what I want to say to you."

She paused, forcing herself to look at his face again. Most of it was wrapped in gauze. Thomas, god, what you did to yourself, she thought. "I thought maybe I should talk to you about Elijah. I thought maybe if we'd talked about Elijah more before, that maybe this wouldn't have happened. See, Elijah was the first boy I ever kissed. My first love. It was impossible for me to feel the same way about you."

Tavia squeezed her eyes shut and let out a sigh. "That came out wrong," she said. She opened her eyes and did a Thomas face check. He still seemed to be asleep. She kept going anyway. "What I mean is that nobody could make me feel the way Elijah did, not you, not anybody, because he was the first. Elijah himself couldn't make me feel the way he did if I met him for the first time now."

Tavia wasn't a hundred percent sure that was true, but she was trying to make a point. "I think maybe you felt inferior to Elijah somehow because you could sense that I'd, that I'd had such strong feelings for him. I never wanted you to feel that way, Thomas. And you know I'm really focused on getting ready for college. You know I wasn't planning to get seriously involved with anybody."

Wait, Tavia told herself. Now you're just trying to make yourself feel better. This is supposed to be about Thomas. "Anyway, anyway, I just wanted to say that spending time with you was great. You're the sweetest guy."

A flash of Thomas accusing her of wanting a white boy filled her head. His face had been twisted with anger. No, more than that, with hatred. She hadn't thought it was possible for Thomas's face to look that way. Suddenly, she heard Seth's voice reading from the diary.

"*It is as if all the citizens are to become Gripped by Madness or taken over by the Devil Himself.*'"

That so perfectly described Thomas. And Tavia bet if she asked Andrea, Andrea would say it described Mrs. Callison too. Is the same thing happening in Raven's Point that happened all those years ago? Tavia wondered. Is that why the birds took me to that little girl's grave, because she lived during the time of the madness?

Tavia began to tremble. She gripped the seat of the plastic chair with both hands. But all that did was start the chair trembling too. There was a way to stop it, she reminded herself. And it must have worked, because Raven's Point turned out okay.

At least until now.

"Hey, Muffin. Hey, woof-woof. Come here, boy," Billy Whitcomb called. "You know me. From the hospital. I've seen you visiting the sick people, you good dog you."

Muffin had a nice neck. Strong looking. Billy wanted to hear it crack. After Muffin spent a little time on the rack, of course.

But Muffin isn't a nuisance, a small voice inside Billy whispered. Muffin made people happy. Maybe Elijah Romano never would have come out of his coma without all those visits from Muffin the therapy dog.

Billy ignored the little voice. Muffin was just a dog. An animal. Animals were put on earth for people to eat, and put to work. And play with.

"Come on, Muffin. Come see your friend Billy."

Muffin took a dump on the Connors' lawn. Then he trotted toward Billy.

Billy crouched down. "That's right. Come right over here."

Muffin crouched down too, low over his front paws, butt in the air, tail wagging. Look at him. "Yeah, you want to play, don't you, buddy. Get over here."

Muffin sprang forward. And locked his teeth on Billy's windpipe. Billy tried to scream, but all that came out was a hiss of air.

Marti unbuttoned another button on her blouse and kept on dancing. She needed this after spending day after day caring for the former coma boy. She needed to keep on dancing. Dancing all by herself, feeling like Britney, feeling like Christina Aguilera. Every guy in the place looking at her, trying to get up the nerve to approach.

Here came a brave boy now, dancing his way up to her. "You look lonely all by yourself."

"I was dancing with that blond guy over there." Marti jerked her chin toward a guy sitting at the bar. "But then he said something rude." She gave a little pout.

"He did, huh?" her dancing partner asked. "Want me to take care of him for you?"

"Would you?" Marti asked. Her brave boy stalked off. A moment later, Marti heard the crack of bone on bone. She didn't bother to check out the action. She danced herself over to Mr. Potbelly, hanging by the jukebox. "The bartender told me he'd give me a free drink if I pulled up my top. I don't think that's very nice, do you?" she asked him.

A minute later, the bartender had a bloody nose. And Marti danced herself on over to one of the lowlifes playing pool. A pool cue could do some serious damage. She might actually watch that action.

Seth sat on the bottom row of the bleachers, holding on to the sensations of that slow dance with Jane. She'd felt so good against him, so—

"McFadden, hello."

Seth looked up and saw Chad standing in front of him. "Hey."

"Hey. I get hey after standing in front of you for fifteen minutes. What were you thinking about so hard?" Chad asked. "You looked constipated." He sat down next to Seth.

"Nothing," Seth answered. "Just waiting for Jane to come out of the bathroom."

"So you came with her, or what?" Chad asked.

"Yeah," Seth answered. He was still trying to keep his Jane sensations. If he talked too much, he was afraid he'd lose them.

"How'd that happen?" Chad asked.

Clearly Chad wasn't going to leave him alone. "The usual way. I asked. She said yes."

"But before that. I didn't even know you knew her," Chad said.

"And you know everything about me, right?" Seth took a swig of his soda.

"Hell, yeah. How else am I going to get my free ride to Duke?" Chad answered. "I got to know everything so I can keep a nice flow of smoke going up your butt."

"I started talking to her one day. She's, I don't know, she's—" Seth didn't know how to describe Jane exactly. It was just that he really liked the way he felt around her. When they talked, she was focused on him. Unlike, say, Andrea, who always seemed to have one eye on her girl friends, like she wanted them to see that she was talking to Seth as much as she wanted to actually talk to him.

"She's?" Chad prompted.

Before Seth could make another attempt at answering, one of the speakers squealed. Seth jerked his head toward the sound just in time to see the speaker crashing off the stage. Chad's father leapt off the stage after it and started kicking the hell out of it.

"He's lost it. Help me get him out of here," Chad said. There was no emotion in his voice. Seth could see he was in crisis-prevention mode—everything focused on dealing with the crap at hand. "Try not to let him see us until we're close enough to grab him."

Mr. Williams slammed his foot through the speaker. Then he reached up and grabbed the microphone off the stage. "Sax," he screeched. "This place is filled with sax. You!" He pointed to a girl wearing a belly shirt. "You should be ashamed of yourself showing off your body like that." He pulled a can of lighter fluid out of his coat pocket and squirted it at the girl.

"All of you should be ashamed," Mr. Williams screamed. He splashed lighter fluid over the crowd. Then he pulled out a box of long wooden kitchen matches.

Forget the sneaking-up plan. There was no time. Seth broke into a run, aiming himself at Mr. Williams. His foot slid over a patch of the lighter fluid, the harsh smell of it filling his lungs. He regained his footing and launched himself at Mr. Williams's knees.

Mr. Williams went down. So did Seth. The matches. Where were the matches? Seth's fingers scrabbled across the slick floor. Yes! There was the hard cardboard of the matchbox. He sent the box spinning across the floor. A second later the can of lighter fluid went bouncing after the box, propelled by a kick from Chad.

"Let's get him out of here." Seth could hear the panic erupting in Chad's voice. Now that the crisis was over, Seth would bet all hell was busting loose inside his friend. He knew that feeling.

"Right," Seth answered. He took Mr. Williams by one elbow. Chad grabbed his father by the other arm. They hauled him to his feet and started toward the door. But it was too late. The cops were already bursting into the gym.

Chapter 9

They and We

Jane moved a little closer to Seth. She wished she could disappear inside him. She was cold, so cold. She knew the gym was heated, and she had her coat on, but it was as if her bones had turned to ice.

"Chad, you want a ride home? Or, I don't know, want to go to the drive-through?" Seth asked.

Chad pulled his gaze away from his father, who was being led out of the gym by the police. "No, I've got to go figure out what the deal is with bail and everything."

"We'll come with you," Jane volunteered. "Or do you want me to call my dad?" Her father and Chad's had been friends forever. When she'd come out of the bathroom and seen that Seth had Mr. Williams pinned to the floor it was like she'd walked into some alternate universe. A cold, dark place. Mr. Williams was the fun dad, the dad who'd play on the slip 'n' slide with you instead of watching, the dad who seemed to remember what it was like to be a kid. And he'd been trying to burn down the gym. A shudder went through Jane's body. Seth wrapped his arm around her and pulled her up against his side. It helped. A little.

"No," Chad answered. "Look, I have to go. I'll talk to you guys later."

"If you think you should, go with him," Jane began.

Seth shook his head. "Sometimes you don't want even your friends around. So, I guess we should go." He slid his arm off her shoulders, and Jane felt the coldness spread from her bones of ice into her flesh, until he took her hand. Then the coldness retreated.

"Yeah," Jane agreed. She concentrated on each step. If she made one wrong move her bones would crack like icicles. Only when she was settled in Seth's car, in their own little world within a world, did she relax her vigilance.

Seth got in the driver's side, slammed the door, put the key in the ignition—and just sat there. "I keep thinking about that journal," he finally said. "Especially that part about the people going insane or being possessed by the devil."

Jane's heart hesitated in her chest, then began beating double time. "I've been thinking about it too. My parents, they've been fighting all the time. Well, they've been fighting a lot for a long time. But, lately . . . " She searched for the right words to express herself. "I don't know, it's like there's something *seething* inside them, some kind of venom. And it keeps coming out. And then tonight, Mr. Williams—"

"I know. The other day at practice, Matthew Plett totally

went off. If he'd been holding a baseball bat, he would have smashed my head to pulp," Seth said. "The guy's usually kind of an a-hole. But not like that."

Jane forced herself to say what she'd been trying to keep herself from thinking. "Do you think it could be happening again? Whatever happened in Raven's Point all those years ago?"

"You want to know why I was doing that research on the history of the island?" Seth asked.

"Tell me," she answered.

"I'm not sure if you'll believe me." Seth turned to her, his blue eyes unreadable in the darkness.

"I promise I'll believe you. Then it will be your turn to believe me. There's some other stuff I haven't told you." Jane leaned closer, needing to see him more clearly.

"Here goes." Seth cleared his throat. "I was going home after practice, and a bunch of—okay, here comes the part that's hard to believe—a bunch of ghosts chased me all the way up to the point. Let me pause here so you can laugh."

"I'm not laughing. I'm kind of creeped out, but I'm definitely not laughing," Jane assured him. God, what was happening in Raven's Point? She wrapped her arms around herself, trying to get warm. Even the little world of San-Jeeth was icing over.

"Anyway, after that, I did some research on ghosts. It seemed like maybe the only way I could get rid of them was to figure out what they wanted," Seth continued. "They were all wearing colonial-style clothes, well, except for this one guy, so I thought I should start digging around in the island's history."

"What was the other guy wearing?" Jane asked. It was the least scary question she had.

"Uh, he was naked," Seth admitted. He laughed. Jane had to laugh too. And for a minute it was like the heater was going full blast. Then Seth said, "Your turn." And the chill invaded Jane's body again.

"For a bunch of days kind of weird stuff has been happening to me," Jane said. "I've been having these time shifts—at least that's what I call them. That or delusions. Or incipient lunacy. Or—"

"You're talking to a guy who has been seeing ghosts," Seth reminded her.

"Right, well, remember how in the library I said I'd heard about a girl who was stoned for being a witch and I thought it was the girl from the diary?" Jane didn't wait for Seth to answer. She rushed on, wanting to get it all out at once. "That wasn't something I heard. It was something I *saw.* I was there, Seth, I swear to god. Somehow I went back in time."

"I believe you," he told her.

"I wish I didn't believe myself," Jane admitted. "There was once I'm pretty sure I went forward in time, I don't know how far, and the whole island had been annihilated. Nothing left but ashes."

"Christ," Seth muttered.

"Yeah." Jane wished she had on gloves and a hat and a muffler and some of those electric socks. But she suspected none of those things would keep her warm. The cold was . . . spiritual. She was soul cold. "Do you think—I don't know, do you think that it means something that we're seeing this stuff? Sometimes I feel like there's a, a *force* controlling the time shifts. Like there is a purpose."

And if that were true, maybe the universe wasn't the pit of madness it seemed. Maybe there was order. A plan, even. Something that cared.

Or something that just wanted to torment her.

"I wish my ghosts had been able to talk," Seth said. "If we knew how things ended up in Raven's Point back then, maybe—"

"Take me to the point," Jane blurted out. Heat flooded her face. It would have felt good if she wasn't dying of humiliation. She knew some people went up to the point to make out, at least when the weather was warmer. "I didn't mean—" Stop. Not one more word, Jane ordered herself. She pulled in a breath and started again. "The time shifts take me to the same place at a different time. At least I know they did on a bunch of the shifts. I'm not sure about a couple. So if we go to the place the ghosts herded you to, maybe I can go back to when they were alive and look around."

"It's too dangerous," Seth told her. "If we go on the theory that the journal is true, Raven's Point was a bad, bad place to be back then."

"The kind of place it might be turning into," Jane said softly. "I appreciate that you're worried about me." And she did, she so did. It made her feel all melty, even when every breath she took in seemed to ice up her nose and throat and lungs. "But if there's any way I could possibly find out something— And, besides, when I go back, it's like I'm watching a 3-D movie or something. No one even sees me." At least most people don't, she added silently, thinking of her younger self and that girl in the one-room school, Mary-Beth.

"I just wish I could go with you," Seth said. He started up the car and pulled out of the lot.

"I do too," Jane answered. This was so weird, and good weird as opposed to the horrible weird that had been happening lately. She hardly knew Seth, it was their first date, but it felt totally normal for him to worry about her, to care about her in this deep way. It's like we've really known each other forever, she thought.

It took only a few minutes to drive to the bottom of the trail leading up to the point. The small-island thing again. Jane scrambled out of the car—if she was going to do this, she needed to do it fast before she wimped out. Ooops. She realized Seth had been coming around to get the door for her. Too late to do anything about it. They started up the cliff, Seth letting Jane set the pace.

"Right here," Seth said when they reached the top.

"Okay. I'm just going to do it, try to," Jane told him. "I always come back at the same time I left. No time passes. So I guess I'll see you in a second."

She shut her eyes. It was hard to concentrate on anything else with Seth there. Take me to 1703, she thought, trusting It to choose the moment, to bring her to the moment in time she needed to see.

Nothing happened. Jane didn't feel a shift. "Sorry," she said, opening her eyes. Seth wasn't there. Jane stood alone on the top of the cliff. I guess this place was pretty much the same, even three hundred years ago, she thought. That's why she hadn't felt the textures of her surroundings change.

Why did It throw me here—now, I mean? Jane wondered. She peered into the darkness. What am I supposed to be seeing? A tiny cracking sound caught her attention. She wasn't alone the way she'd thought. Jane turned toward the sound. It could have been made by an animal, she guessed.

No. A girl was hiding against the huge oak tree, her body pressed tightly against the rough bark. Jane realized the girl was Mary-Beth, the one who'd been able to see her the last time.

"Don't be scared," Jane said. "I'm not going to hurt you."

"Devil!" Mary-Beth shouted. She reached into her pocket, drew out a small, wickedly sharp dagger, and lunged at Jane.

"No!" Jane shouted. Too late. The blade had entered her flesh. And . . . and so had Mary-Beth's arm.

Jane's bones began to crackle. She could feel them moving inside her, shrinking. And her hair was twisting this way and that. Something thick wrapped itself around her legs.

"Where are you, devil?" Mary-Beth shouted. Jane's mouth opened and shut along with the words.

Footsteps raced toward her. "Mary-Beth, what is it?"

Jane turned, and a guy around her age rushed up to her. The gray-eyed boy she'd seen in the one-room school. Wait. Weird. He was staring right at her and he didn't seem scared.

"I saw a devil! It appeared right out of the air!" Again Jane's mouth moved with the words Mary-Beth was speaking. Where was Mary-Beth? Jane could hear her, but she couldn't see her.

The boy glanced around nervously. "You most likely fell asleep waiting for me," he said, speaking directly to Jane. He reached out and took her hand.

I'm in Mary-Beth's body, Jane realized. When we touched, I got sucked inside. She could feel Mary-Beth's long skirt around her legs and Mary-Beth's braids hanging down her back. She reached up to touch one of them—or tried to. But she had no control of Mary-Beth's body.

What if I can't get out? Jane thought wildly. What if I'm stuck in here for the rest of my life? I mean the rest of hers.

"I wasn't asleep, Joshua. I know full well when I'm asleep," Mary-Beth insisted.

Joshua! Jane knew that name from Maureen's diary. She stared at the guy—face all sharp angles, body long and lean. This was him, the one Maureen told how to stop the evil. That's why I'm here, Jane thought. I have to find out what Joshua knows.

"It's cold. Let's gather up some wood," Joshua told Mary-Beth. "Emily and Noah should be here any time."

"Don't try to distract me like I'm an infant." Mary-Beth planted her hands on her hips. "I'm only a year younger than you are."

"It's cold. That's all I'm saying," Joshua replied. "Besides, with the fire, we'll have light. It will make the demon easier to see if it reappears."

"Maybe it will keep it away entirely," Mary-Beth said. "I've heard tell that demons can only live in darkness."

Jane knew what Mary-Beth was doing. Mary-Beth was hoping to make her desire come true by speaking it aloud—

say the demons can't live in the light and they can't. Jane had tried the technique herself. And it didn't work.

Mary-Beth strode toward the closest tree and began gathering an armload of fallen branches. Jane's hands moved purposefully without her control. It's not your body, Jane reminded herself.

"Leave the bigger branches. I'll fetch them," Joshua instructed.

Mary-Beth immediately grabbed the biggest branch in sight. Jane felt her—their—back muscles protest as Mary-Beth dragged her load to the center of the clearing.

Show-off, Jane thought. Mary-Beth cut a glance at Joshua and Jane realized who she was showing off for.

"I see you have Mary-Beth doing most of the work," a male voice called. Mary-Beth turned her head, and Jane saw a beefy boy with a broad smile coming toward them. A girl with her black hair in a low knot followed close behind.

"I told you to leave the big ones for me," Joshua snapped. "Go on and tell Noah that."

"Joshua told me to leave the kindling for him because he knows how to pick the very best twigs," Mary-Beth answered.

She's flirting with him, Jane realized. Teasing-flirting. And he's oblivious, she thought, watching Joshua sputter about how it absolutely wasn't true. Poor girl.

"Well, if Josh gets the kindling and Mary-Beth gets the logs, I suppose I'll have to sit on this rock and look pretty," the girl said.

But she didn't sit down. She headed to a huge log at one edge of the clearing and grinned at Mary-Beth. Mary-Beth ran over to her, and together they rolled the log over to the boys.

"As always, you win," Noah told the girl. "But I think that log's better for sitting on than burning." He plopped down on it. "How am I at sitting and looking pretty, Emily?"

Emily. That's the name of the girl Tavia was researching, Jane thought. Things were converging. It, whatever It was, had sent her to the right moment.

"You'll get no compliments from me," Emily told Noah.

"Are you certain?" Noah grabbed Emily by the waist and pulled her down on his lap. "Not one little compliment?"

"Stop that foolishness while I light the fire." Joshua took out a flint and used it to light the kindling in several places.

"Why did you want to meet here tonight?" Emily asked. She slid off Noah's lap, the smile fading from her face.

Joshua didn't answer. He added some larger branches. The bonfire's blaze leapt tall.

"Josh," Noah prodded. "Tell us. We can all see there's something wrong."

"Something new," Mary-Beth added. She sat down on the large rock near the fire. "I don't know how there can possibly be something new, but there is, isn't there?"

"You all know bad things have been happening in our village," Joshua began, eyes on the fire.

"Of course we know that!" Emily burst out. "The witch

made my own papa kill my mother. Do you think because I smile or laugh that I have possibly forgotten!"

Noah pulled Emily close against him. "No one thinks that."

"Maureen wasn't a witch," Joshua said, each word coming out slowly and deliberately.

"Have you lost your brains?" Noah demanded. "We all know what she's done. She magicked Mrs. Adams into burning down the Langly's house. And it's said that—" He hesitated, glancing from Mary-Beth to Emily. "That Phoebe Comstalk is going to have her father's babe. Everyone on the island has a story to tell. The witch was mightily powerful."

Jane shivered. No, Mary-Beth shivered and Jane felt it. Although she knew she'd be shivering herself if she were in her own body.

"The evil, 'tis still happening," Joshua interrupted. "Maureen is dead and 'tis still happening. Can't you see that?"

Mary-Beth chewed the inside of her cheek, and Jane tasted the salty-sweet blood. "Today I saw old Mr. Leary. He was stripped naked and he was using his knife to skin himself. 'Twas as if he was a deer he had killed." Hot bile mixed with the blood in Mary-Beth's mouth, and Jane felt their shared stomach heave.

"Yet the witch—as you call her—has been dead these three days," Joshua pointed out. "She couldn't have made Mr. Leary do such a thing to himself."

"There is some logic to what you say," Noah admitted, his green eyes narrowed. "Must be there is another witch on the island. We have to hunt her down—"

"No," Joshua interrupted. "That's not how to stop it. That's not how to save those who have survived this far."

"How then?" Emily demanded. "That's why you brought us here, isn't it? To tell us? Speak then, Joshua."

He's afraid to tell them, Jane thought. One look in his eyes and you can see he's terrified.

"One-eye Maureen—" Joshua began.

"The witch!" Emily interrupted him.

"She wasn't a witch," Joshua said. "But she could see things, things that were going to happen."

"But couldn't only a witch do that?" Noah jumped in. The firelight leapt across his face, making him look only half human.

"Maureen was visited by a white raven. 'Twas the one who showed her things," Joshua continued, ignoring Noah. "It showed her all the horrible deeds that would be done in our village. But the raven also showed her a way to stop the evil who now lives among us."

"We're here because of something a bird showed a witch?" Noah spat out.

"Would you rather go home?" Joshua burst out. "Caleb will hurt you if you do. Maureen told me."

"Caleb is my brother," Noah answered, the words coming out soft and weak.

Noah is already afraid of his brother, Jane thought. Something had already happened.

"I believe what Maureen told me. Everything she told me," Joshua went on. "If we do not have the courage to stop the evil, everyone in Raven's Point will die."

Jane felt Mary-Beth's heart begin to beat faster. "We're supposed to fight the demons?" she asked.

"Maureen didn't call it a demon. She called it evil," Joshua explained. "And she didn't say we had to fight it, not exactly. What Maureen said was that we had to let the evil into ourselves and then trap it inside."

"Let the demons inside us?" Mary-Beth's voice cracked as she asked the question.

"That's madness," Noah burst out. "Mayhap Maureen was a witch. Mayhap she wasn't. But that is madness."

"What's happening in our village is madness," Joshua countered. "I don't know about you, but this isn't a place I want to live. To be honest, I don't think 'tis a place anyone will be *able* to live for long. The . . . evilness won't be satisfied until we're all dead. Then Maureen thought it would move on, to another island, to more people."

"Why us?" Emily cried. "Why should we have to do this?"

Joshua shrugged. "All I know is Maureen said it had to be the four of us, no one else." He swallowed hard. Jane could see his Adam's apple move up and down. "There's something else. I didn't know if I should tell you . . . "

"Tell us everything," Noah demanded, his hands balling into fists. "You have no right to keep anything from us."

"Maureen said if things went wrong, if we . . . if we die, we will be reborn, many years from now. We will have other lives, here on the island. And in that life, we will have gifts that we can use to battle the evil if it ever comes again," Joshua concluded in a rush.

Jane felt as if she'd been struck by lightning. I'm Mary-

Beth, she realized. That's why she can see me, just the way my younger self could see me. They can see me because they *are* me. I'm the reincarnation of Mary-Beth.

"I have to say that's not much of a comfort." Emily picked up a pinecone and threw it into the fire. It crackled and hurled sparks into the night.

"I'm going home," Noah said. He sprang up from the log. "This is nonsense. 'Tis devil lies."

"Mayhap!" Joshua exclaimed. "But if there is a chance that we can stop the evil, mustn't we do it?"

"I'm going home," Noah repeated, pacing around the fire.

"To what?" Joshua asked softly. "To Caleb? You know how jealous he is of your mother's attentions. He fumes every time she calls you her baby. Do you know what he wants to do, Noah? What he *will* do? If you go back home, in two days' time, he will cut out your heart and burn it."

He looked at Emily. "And you. You've seen how your father keeps sharpening his ax, sharpening it while his eyes are on your neck. Do you want to go back down the hill to him?" He moved his gaze to Mary-Beth. "Maureen saw that your dog would turn on you. He's already killed your sister's kitten, hasn't he?"

Jane felt tears sting in Mary-Beth's eyes. Mary-Beth nodded.

Believe him, Mary-Beth. Believe him, believe him, believe him. Jane tried to inject her thoughts into Mary-Beth's head. Whatever these four had done, it had worked. At least for hundreds of years the evil had been put to rest.

"I'm staying. I'll do it," Mary-Beth vowed, her eyes

locked on Joshua's, drawing strength from him, and letting him draw strength from her.

Emily reached out and took Mary-Beth's hand. "Every day there is a new atrocity," Emily said. "You're right, Joshua. It's no place to live. There's nothing to go back to."

"Maureen was right about so much," Joshua said. He took Emily's hand in his and reached to Noah. "Why would she be wrong about this?"

Noah met Joshua's gaze for a long moment. "I think she was right about Caleb." He took Joshua's hand. "What exactly are we to do?"

"The evil has no body of its own, at least not yet," Joshua answered. "Maureen said if it grew strong enough it would be able to obtain its own form. What we must do is invite it into our bodies and when we feel it inside us, we must lock it there, as if we were prisons of stone."

"I don't understand," Mary-Beth said. Jane didn't understand either.

"That was all she said," Joshua confessed. "She said that we would understand once it was inside."

"And how do we call it?" Noah asked.

Mary-Beth's teeth began to chatter. Emily squeezed her hand more tightly.

"We stare into the fire and we think about the things the evil has done, and we wish for it to be inside us." Noah took a step closer to the blaze, tugging the other three with him.

"Now?" Emily asked.

"I'll count to three," Noah answered. "One . . . two . . . three."

Mary-Beth locked her eyes on the flames. Evil being, come inside me, she thought. Jane heard the thought as if it were her own. She tried to add her own mental push behind it.

The flames of the bonfire thinned and lengthened. Mary-Beth gasped—and one of the snakes of fire entered her mouth. Down her throat it swept, Mary-Beth and Jane fighting not to gag. Then Jane felt the boiling snake wrap around their ribs and touch their frantically beating heart.

The image of a younger Mary-Beth under a down comforter, her mother kissing her forehead, flashed into the brain Mary-Beth and Jane shared. Jane felt as if she were floating on a cloud of satin in a starry sky. Safe.

The snake shifted and a new image appeared—Mary-Beth floating on her back in a stream, eyes closed. Jane's world became cool and buoyant. Pure pleasure.

The snake shifted again. A new emotion took over Jane. Jealousy. The image of Jonah stealing a kiss from a girl holding a red rose in her hand.

The colors brightened, the dark blue of the girl's dress so deep and rich Jane wanted to lick it, the red of the rose so bright it dazzled. The jealousy Jane felt intensified along with the image. Overwhelming her. Consuming her.

The emotion was like gasoline to the snake of flame. It grew. And began to climb back up Jane's throat. A hundred times stronger.

Mary-Beth! Don't let it out! Jane silently screamed.

Mary-Beth squeezed her eyes shut. She clamped her teeth together. She curled her hands into tight fists.

The snake was trapped. It exploded inside Mary-Beth.

And Mary-Beth began to burn from the inside out. Her intestines shriveling. Her heart charring. Her ribs turning to charcoal.

Angry white blisters filled with pus erupted on Jane's body and she let out a shriek of agony.

Seth reached for her, but there was no place he could touch without hurting her even more.

Then as fast as they'd appeared, the blisters were gone. Jane's skin faded from red to its usual cream in seconds. "What the hell happened?" he cried.

Jane threw herself against him. He wrapped his arms tight around her, feeling tremors racing through her. "It's okay," he whispered. "I'm here. I'm here. You're okay."

The tremors slowed. Then stopped. But Seth didn't let Jane go. He began to gently stroke her hair. "Tell me," he said, keeping up the slow rhythm.

"They were so young," Jane said, her voice muffled against his chest. She lifted her face and looked up at him. "I only want to have to say it once. We need to find Tavia."

"Okay. In a minute, in a minute," Seth said. He couldn't let Jane go, not yet. It was as if he'd almost lost a piece of himself.

Tavia stared at the Romano's house, stared up at Elijah's lit window. He was there. He was awake. She could get out of the car, go to the door, knock, and a moment later she'd be with him.

But was that what she wanted?

Talking to Thomas, well, talking *at* Thomas, had

brought back so many feelings. I tried to tape them up in that box with all my little mementos, she thought. But they were too strong. When she'd told Thomas that Elijah was her first love, it sounded so neat and tidy. It was something she'd been through, something very special. Something that was past.

But if she was going to face the truth—finally—she had to admit that Elijah was her love. Period. Not a first love to be remembered fondly. Her one and only love. There was nobody else she'd feel that way about.

Tavia forced herself to look away from Elijah's light. If you go in there, that's it. Right now, you can still stagger away, she told herself. You can be sensible. You can do all the things you've planned. You can meet someone else someday and probably even be happy in a calm kind of way.

Or you can go in there. To him. Because he needs you, and you know it. Something's wrong, and he needs you. And maybe you won't be able to have the perfect college resume, or win every meet and still be there for him. It's time to choose.

A knock on her car window jerked Tavia away from her thoughts. She rolled down the window. "Can we get in for a minute?" Elijah's sister asked, gesturing to Seth McFadden, who stood beside her. "We need to talk to you, but it can't be in the house."

Tavia reached over and unlocked the passenger door. Jane and Seth crowded into the front seat with her. Tavia's skin began to tingle in a way that was almost painful, like she was standing under a shower with that needle-point spray. "What's going on?" she asked. She couldn't come up with one reason the two of them could have for talking to her. Jane, yes, she might have wanted to talk to Tavia about Elijah. But the two of them—Tavia was baffled.

"I'm just going to spit this out. There's no intro I can give that would help," Jane said. She reached over and grabbed Tavia's hand, startling her. "Tavia, you know that girl you were interested in researching—Emily?"

"Emily Robertson," Tavia answered. The tingling intensified. Now it had almost an electric buzz.

"Well, I know how she died. She coaxed this evil being into her body, and it burned her to a crisp," Jane said in a rush. "Her and three other kids." Jane turned to Seth. "That's what I saw when I went back in time."

Tavia pulled her hand away from Jane. "What?"

"I went back in time. That's my gift," Jane answered. "I think Seth's is the ability to see ghosts. Okay, I have to back up a little bit. I'm not doing this very well."

"You're doing great," Seth told her.

"A few days ago, weird stuff began happening to me and Seth," Jane explained. "I started being pushed back in time. Different years at different times. And Seth started seeing ghosts, ghosts he thinks were trying to tell him something. If I'm right, some kind of weirdness has probably been happening to you too."

"The animals," Tavia whispered.

"What?" Jane demanded. She grabbed Tavia's hand again. "Please tell us. Don't be afraid. We won't think you're crazy. We're all in this together."

"I—" Tavia hesitated. But it would feel so good to talk

to somebody about what had been happening. "I was out for a run," she rushed on before she could censor herself. "And I was thinking something like 'go, faster, run.' Then all these animals came out of everywhere, running with me. I thought maybe earthquake or fire or some kind of predator. But when I stopped, they stopped."

"Unbelievable," Seth said. "But not. Considering."

"It's happened other times too. I can sort of tell animals what I want, and they'll do it." It sounded completely ridiculous, but Seth and Jane didn't laugh.

"So that's your gift, communicating with animals," Jane told her.

"Go back to the gift thing," Seth said. "You didn't really explain it."

"I know. I guess it's so hideous I don't even want to think about it. But let me spew. And don't interrupt, okay? I just want to get it out." Jane hauled in a long breath. "The three of us have lived before. We died in 1703. I was a girl named Mary-Beth." She turned to Tavia. "And you were Emily."

That's why the birds brought me to her grave, Tavia thought. You're insane, she immediately told herself. You can't be believing this. But was reincarnation actually harder to believe than being flown to the cemetery by a flock of birds?

"I don't know who you were, Seth. There were two boys, Joshua and Noah. You were one of them. Joshua I think. Joshua's the Joshua from the diary we read. Remember how the girl who wrote it, Maureen, said that she'd told Joshua how to fight the evil. Well, the way to stop it was for Joshua and three other kids—Emily, Mary-Beth, and Noah—to try and trap the evil, the evil she wrote about, inside themselves. But Maureen also told them that if they failed, they'd have other lives, in the future. And that in those lives they'd have gifts they would be able to use to fight the evil if it ever returned."

"Fight the evil," Seth repeated.

Jane reached out and took his hand. The electric buzz running through Tavia increased, as if Seth had just added power to the generator. All the tiny hairs on her arms and the back of her neck stood up.

"Yeah, fight the evil," Jane said.

"I believe you," Tavia admitted. "Things are happening in Raven's Point, horrible evil things. And what's been happening with the animals is strange enough to make me believe almost anything."

"At least the four of us were given powers so this time we could really battle it," Jane said. "Maybe if we find a way to combine all our gifts we can kill the evil, whatever it is, together."

All the saliva evaporated from Tavia's mouth. She had to swallow hard before she could speak. "There's only one problem. The evil's already here. And there are only three of us."

The electric current was back. It seemed to be racing back and forth from Tavia's hand to Jane's.

Aaaah. I stretch. My new body is a new universe. I stretch. The transfer has weakened me. But I am much closer to my prey. I easily walk among them. They love my kind. They pet me, feed me scraps of their own food, let me sleep on their beds. I will grow strong here in this body.

And when I am ready to transfer again . . . Yes. Aaaah. I will be inside my prey. I will control my food. I will drain every drop of hate and envy and anger. Some are easy to find. I reach in, and it is there waiting for me. A touch and it flows like blood from a wound. Some I have to work for. Fear can easily be twisted into the emotions I crave. And even in love there are always tiny veins of fear, anger, envy, and sometimes even hate itself. All I need to do is squeeze these veins until they taint the love. Then I can consume it all, growing stronger and stronger.

Until I will no longer need a host. Then I will have my own body once more. And I will stretch. And I will feed. And I will destroy. Then I will stretch again.

Chapter 10

Jane, Seth, and Terry Freakin' Rheingold

Seth pulled into the 7-Eleven parking lot on the way to school the next morning. On his way inside, he grabbed one of the red plastic baskets by the door. Then he headed for the Pop-Tarts.

Friggin' coward. Friggin' weakling. Friggin' a-hole.

Seth reached the Pop-Tarts and started loading his basket.

Friggin' coward. Friggin' weakling. Friggin' a-hole. The thoughts were like bullets in his brain. But he couldn't keep them from coming. They'd been blasting him all night.

Seth strode up to the counter and dumped out his Pop-Tarts. "I'm gonna get some more stuff. I'll be back," he told the cashier.

Friggin' coward. Friggin' weakling. Friggin' a-hole.

Seth swept out his arm and knocked the remaining Pop-Tarts boxes into his basket. Wasn't gonna be enough.

There might not be enough in the whole damn place. He reached out and grabbed the first thing his fingers touched. A loaf of bread. Fine.

How am I supposed to help save the world or whatever? Seth thought. He threw another loaf of Wonder bread into his basket. I'm not that guy. Ask Terry freakin' Rheingold.

Seth's basket was almost full again. He jammed in a couple of packages of Hostess cupcakes, a package of SnoBalls, some of those minidonuts.

Friggin' coward. Friggin' weakling. Friggin' a-hole.

"Seth, hi."

Crap. It was Jane. The last person he wanted to see right now.

The only person he needed to see.

Seth caught Jane's gaze flick down to the basket full of garbage. "My turn to bring breakfast for the team. Come on. I'll drive you to school." He dropped the basket, took Jane by the arm, and hustled her out the door and into his car.

"You didn't buy your stuff," Jane said. "What about the team?"

"Screw them," Seth burst out. Jane raised her eyebrows. "Sorry," Seth muttered. "It's just— I don't know if I can do this, okay? I'm not the guy. I shouldn't be the guy." He knew he was coming across half crazy, but he couldn't help it.

"You're scared," Jane said softly. She reached out and covered one of his hands with hers. He realized he was shaking, not just his hand, his whole body. He'd lost it. Completely lost it. He couldn't stop seeing it. That day with

Terry. What he'd done. Christ. He was nobody's hero. There was no way he could do anything to help the town. He was a killer. A murderer.

Friggin' coward. Friggin' weakling. Friggin' a-hole.

"I'm scared too," Jane admitted. "We're all scared. And it's not like I'm some Buffy type. God, I can't even keep my parents from going at each other." She sucked in a breath and rushed on. "But we can stop it, Seth. It's going to be different this time. We'll find the fourth, and we have powers, and we'll come up with a plan and—"

"You'll be better off without me," Seth told her. He ripped his hand away from her grasp. "I'll only screw it up."

"Why would you say that?" Jane cried out. She looked at him, trusting even now, hopeful.

"Why would I say that?" Seth repeated. "I'll tell you why." And then it will be over, he thought. And then she'll never want to look at me again. Forget about touching me.

"I'm a killer, okay?" Seth told Jane, speaking slowly so she wouldn't be able to miss a word. "I murdered my best friend."

"If you want to go, go," Seth told her. "It's okay." He said it like she was out the car and halfway down the block already.

And there was a part of Jane that wanted to be exactly there. Just away from Seth. She had enough to deal with. Was she supposed to take on more and more and more until she collapsed?

But she couldn't leave him. She barely knew the guy, but

there were these threads between them. No, not threads, more like veins. Jane didn't know how it happened so fast, but she was connected to Seth. If she got out of the car right now, those veins that had formed between them would burst. She didn't think she'd survive that.

"What happened?" she asked.

"I told you. I killed my best friend. What else is there to say?" Seth spat out. He grabbed the steering wheel with both hands. It didn't stop him from shaking.

"I think there's a lot more to say," Jane answered. Impulsively, she grabbed one of Seth's hands and held it tightly in both of hers. The shudders moved through his body and into hers. "What happened?" she repeated.

How could she still be sitting there? Holding his hand for chrissake? Seth thought.

But she was. And she wanted to know, she wanted him to talk, she didn't expect him to pretend it never happened the way his parents did.

"I was six," he began. He heard Jane draw in a sharp breath, but he didn't look at her. If he was going to do this, he had to say it all without stopping. "I was six," he repeated.

"You fight like a girl!" Terry yelled. He grabbed a pillow off Seth's bed and whacked him with it.

Seth gave an animal cry and leapt up on the bed. He snatched up his other pillow and slammed it into Terry's head. "You're the girl. You're wearing a skirt. Terry's wearing a little skirt."

"You're wearing a skirt!" Terry yelled back. "I'm tap-dancing on your skirt!" Terry grabbed Seth around the

knees and hauled him off the bed. He got Seth pinned by sitting on him. "Computer keys!" Terry shouted.

"No!" Seth yelled back, already laughing.

Terry started poking Seth's chest with two fingers. "Computer keys!" he cried. It was like tickling but harder. Every time someone gave Seth computer keys he laughed until he started to choke. And Terry knew it.

Terry started poking Seth's chest faster. "I'm gonna puke," Seth warned him. "I'm gonna puke all over your head."

"Say 'I'm a girl,'" Terry ordered. "Say 'My name is Sethalina and I wear a little tank top.'"

"No way!" Seth started making puking noises. He made really great puking noises. He practiced them in the bathtub. "I'm gonna do it. I'm gonna spew all over your head."

"Guys!" his mother called up the stairs. "I can hear you all the way in the laundry room. Keep it down, okay?"

Terry stopped poking for a minute. Got you now, Seth thought. He flipped Terry onto his back and pinned him. "Sorry, Mom," Seth yelled. "We'll be quiet." He started poking Terry's chest. "Computer keys, computer keys," he whispered.

"I'm gonna puke," Terry whispered back.

"Copycat." Seth kept poking, fast and hard. That was the best way to do computer keys.

"No, really. I'm gonna puke. Time-out!" Terry begged.

Terry actually had puked once when they were playing. It was pretty gross.

"One minute time-out," Seth said. "But then, no mercy." He slid off Terry.

"Psych!" Terry cried.

Terry'd fooled him. Terry could always fool him. "You are going to be so sorry," Seth warned him.

"I'm shakin'. I'm peeing my pants," Terry answered.

"You will be," Seth shot back. He ran into his parents' bedroom and opened the big closet. Something to stand on. He needed something to stand on. Seth stacked three suitcases on top of each other and climbed up them. He felt around on the top shelf. He knew it was up there. He wasn't supposed to know, but he did. Terry really is gonna pee when he sees this, Seth thought.

His fingers connected with the cardboard box. A second later he had what he was looking for. It was heavier than he thought it would be, the metal cool in his hand. "You're gonna pee, Terry!" he yelled.

Then he was racing back to his room, the gun in his hand. He skidded to a stop in the doorway, then aimed the gun at Terry. "Now, you say it. 'My name is Teresa and I wear a cute little tank top.' Say it."

"That thing is cool," Terry said.

"It's my dad's," Seth told him. "Bang!" he shouted.

"You're supposed to pull the trigger, hair ball," Terry said. "Let me hold it. You don't even know how."

"Yes I do!" Seth protested. He slid his finger around the trigger. "Bang!" he shouted as he pulled the trigger back.

"And then I was on my butt," Seth continued. "I actually flew backward. And my ears were ringing. The sound was so loud. Not like on TV. Then I stood up. But Terry didn't. He was laying there. I told him to stop screwing around. But I knew he wasn't. You ever see a dead body?"

Jane shook her head.

"You just know. The life is gone, and you just know. And I knew, but I went up and started shaking him, screaming at him to stop messing around. Then my mom was there, and she pulled me off and . . . "

Seth pulled in a deep, shuddering breath. It seemed like he just realized that he'd been crying the whole time he told her the story. He yanked his hand away from hers and wiped his face with his sleeve. "And that's it. That's the deal." The words came out harsh and clipped. "After all the legal stuff was over, we moved to Sacramento. Everyone in the old neighborhood knew. Everyone was talking about it. Then my dad got a job offer on Raven's Point. And I ended up here."

"It was an accident," Jane said softly. "You—"

"I pointed a gun at my best friend and pulled the trigger," Seth interrupted. He put the key in the ignition and started the car. "We should get to school."

"No!" Jane burst out. "No. I have to go somewhere first. Will you take me?" She didn't wait for him to answer. "Just head toward the marina."

Seth followed her instructions. But he didn't look at her. He hadn't looked at her since he'd finished telling her what happened that day. It's like he'd trusted her enough to tell her, but now he wished he hadn't.

"Turn right at the corner," Jane said. She hoped she wasn't doing something stupid. But she had to try to find a way to make Seth see.

"Okay, now just park right here," Jane told Seth. "Now

look at those kids." She pointed to the playground of the elementary school. "I'm pretty sure those are first-graders. Look at them. Look how little they are. Seth, that's how old you were when you accidentally shot Terry. You were just a little boy."

Jane glanced over at him. Did he get it? Was he able to take it in at all? She couldn't tell. He was staring at the playground, but his blue eyes were flat as a doll's eyes.

"You were playing, right? Just like those two boys." She jerked her head toward two kids pretending to fight with light sabers.

"Except the gun was real," Seth said. His voice was flat too.

"Yeah, it was real. And when you were the age of those little kids you totally got that," Jane answered. She forced herself to go further, to really hurt Seth if that's what it took. "You knew that it was loaded. You knew what a bullet would do fired at such close range. You knew that blood would come spewing out of Terry. You knew he'd fall down dead right in front of you. You knew his parents—"

"No!" Seth blurted out.

"No?" Jane challenged, turning toward him. He met her gaze for the first time since he'd finished his story.

"No," Seth repeated. "I wasn't thinking like that. I was just thinking Terry would think the gun was cool. I wasn't . . . I didn't . . . "

"I know," Jane told him. She wanted to take his hand again, but she thought he might jerk it away like he had before.

"But Terry's still dead," Seth said.

"I know," Jane answered. She turned her attention back to the playground. "When I was their age, I was such a little goof," she commented, figuring that maybe it was time to take a break from the intense stuff. "I used to pretend that the baseball backstop was a spaceship. I'd bounce against it three times, and then I'd be on the planet Gloopus where I was a princess and rode a unicorn."

"Gloopus, huh?" Seth sounded a little more . . . more human. More alive.

"Sometimes, after school, when none of his friends were around I'd get Elijah to play with me too," Jane continued. "He was a good big brother. Is," she corrected herself.

"What the hell?" Seth burst out. "Do you see that?" He didn't wait for Jane to answer. He jumped out of the car, raced over to the chain-link fence around the playground, and vaulted over it.

A second later, Jane understood why. Three little girls were throwing rocks at a fourth. Throwing them hard. The little girl being attacked was crouched on the ground with her arms locked over her head.

Jane scrambled out of the car and climbed the fence. Then she tore after Seth. "What are you girls doing?" she cried. She grabbed the first girl that she came to and held her by the shoulders. She glared at the other two girls, trying to control them with a look.

Seth had the little girl they'd been attacking in his arms. Crimson blood was running down her forehead and across her white face. "Take her to the nurse," Jane told him. "It's in the smaller building to the left." He sprinted away the second the words left her mouth.

"You're Jim Johansson's little sister, aren't you?" Jane asked the girl she still held by the shoulders. "Josie, right?"

"JoJo." The little girl twisted out of Jane's grip. "You shouldn't have stopped us. Lily's a big, stinky baby. She still wears diapers at night. That's because she wets the bed."

"And what? That makes it okay for you to throw rocks at her?" Jane demanded.

The two other little girls looked at the ground. But JoJo looked straight up into Jane's face. "Yes. She doesn't have any more good toys left. She should just be dead."

Jane felt as if she'd just downed five glasses of ice water in a row. Her belly ached. And she was so cold. Cold on the inside.

"JoJo, Lee, Bonnie. I need all three of you to come with me," Ms. Paddock called as she strode toward them. She doesn't look that different, Jane thought. She'd had Ms. Paddock as her second grade teacher.

"I'm glad you were here, Jane," Ms. Paddock said, then she turned her attention to the little girls. "Follow me," she ordered. "And no talking."

Jane watched them until they disappeared into one of the classrooms. "*She should just be dead.*" JoJo's words slid around in Jane's head. "*She should just be dead.*" JoJo had spoken so matter-of-factly. Like it was no big thing. Just something that needed to happen.

If Lucy and the others had had rocks in the bathroom the other night, they would have been throwing them at me, Jane thought. Everyone is changing. Everyone is rotting.

And I'm supposed to stop it. Me and Seth and Tavia and . . . someone.

Seth loped up to Jane, pulling her away from her thoughts. "The little girl, Lily, she's going to be okay. She's unconscious, but she's going to be okay."

"It was no kind of accident," Jane told him. "Those little girls wanted her dead."

"It's the madness." Seth raked his fingers through his dark hair. "So I guess we have a world to save. We've got to stop this thing while it's still contained on the island."

And hearing Seth say that, it was like drinking hot tea. The coldness retreated from her body. "What do you think our first step should be?"

"I'm thinking maybe I'll ask for help from an old friend," Seth answered.

Seth gave Jane a wave, then walked down the pier. The marina was deserted at this time of day, all the boats already out. And deserted was what he needed. He sat down at the end of the pier facing the water, legs dangling. "Terry Rheingold. Come to me!" he shouted.

"Geez, I'm right here. You don't have to shout," Terry answered. And he was right there—sitting next to Seth. "So do you think you can finally get over your I-killed-my-best-friend bullshit? 'Cause Jane's right. It was an accident. And you know it, hair ball."

"It doesn't matter. I still—"

Terry slapped Seth on the side of the head. "You don't have time for that crap anymore," he said. "You have new crap you have to deal with. A big stinking pile of it."

"Yeah. That's why I called you. You know about, I don't know, the other realm or whatever, right? I thought maybe you could tell me what we're supposed to do to fight the evil taking over everyone. Or even just who the fourth is."

"I got no idea. Nothing to do with me," Terry said. "I'm here because of you. That's it."

"What?" Seth burst out.

"I can't cross over or whatever you want to call it because you're holding me here," Terry answered. "Are you about ready to let it go? 'Cause spending every minute with you is getting real old. Especially the whole Pop-Tart thing. Nasty. If you have to scarf and barf why not use Cheetos or something. Seeing you puke orange would be more entertaining. Or, hey, maybe—"

"Shut up," Seth mumbled.

Terry gasped. "You're telling me, the poor little boy you killed, to shut up?"

Seth smiled. He couldn't stop himself. It was kind of like he was six again, just hanging with Terry. "I'm telling you to shut the hell up."

"I'd fight you for that, except you fight like a girl," Terry told him. "A little tank-top-wearing girl."

"I'd tap-dance on your skirt." Seth snorted. "How did we come up with that one anyway? Tap-dance on your skirt. It's not very macho."

"Hey, we were six," Terry answered.

"Yeah," Seth agreed. And it felt as if his chest had gotten pumped full of helium. Like he could just float into the air any second. Stay focused, he told himself. "So there's nothing you can tell me about how we're supposed to save the town or whatever?"

"I'm thinking the ghosts who chased you up that hill

were trying to tell you something," Terry answered. "Ghost communication isn't that easy. I can talk to you, because we're friends. But even I can't talk to the other ghosts that well." Terry stood up. "I'll give it a shot, though. Maybe charades. I was always kick-ass at charades."

"Even if we just knew where the evil was centered, if it even is, that would help," Seth said.

"Put your Dr. Doolittle to work on that. Animals can sense things," Terry suggested. "And I'll get back to you with what I find out from the other Caspers."

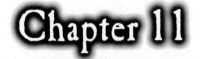

Chapter 11

The Source

I had the weirdest dream last night," Tavia said as she touched up her lipstick. She made sure to talk loudly enough so that everyone in the locker room could hear her. "I was standing next to this huge bonfire up on the point. Three other kids were with me and we all just went up in flames." She glanced around, trying to gauge if anybody's ears were perking up.

"That's not so weird," someone called from the next row of lockers. "I dreamed I was a cafeteria lady and my hair was really long and I couldn't keep it all in the hairnet and it got in all the food and everyone yelled at me."

"Oh gross," Olivia Cavenaugh said. She slammed her locker shut. "I didn't need to hear that right before lunch."

There's got to be a better way to find the fourth, Tavia thought. A *faster* way. Because there wasn't much time left. She could feel it, feel the madness growing. It was like a high-pitched whine in her ears.

She loitered, letting the locker room clear out. She needed a few minutes alone. Just a few. She had more hints to drop, more reactions to watch. But it had gotten so she could hardly breathe around other people. She had to be so wary. Any one of them could be affected, could be incubating the madness inside them.

When the only sound in the locker room was the drip of a shower that hadn't been turned all the way off, Tavia sat down on the wooden bench in front of her locker. She closed her eyes and started to go through her relaxation routine. Toes, tighten, tighten, tighten, then release. Calves tighten, tighten, tighten, then release. Thighs—

Her eyes popped open. The dripping water, it seemed to be forming words. She stood up and moved toward the showers. The soft, soft words became clearer. "Can't. Dirty. Can't." Now the voice sounded human.

Tavia stepped into the shower room. "Who's in here?" she called.

No answer. Just the whispers. "Can't. Can't." Tavia followed the sounds. She found Grace Harding curled up in the corner of the last shower stall. Her sweats were soaked through, her curly brown hair dripping, and she was trembling.

Grace curled up tighter, like she wanted to disappear entirely, as Tavia crouched down next to her. "What's wrong?" Tavia asked.

"I kept washing. But . . ." Grace shook her head, clumps of wet hair falling over her face.

"But what?" Tavia prompted.

"Not clean," Grace answered, the words muffled because her face was pressed against her knees.

"You look clean to me. Let me get you some towels. You have to be freezing," Tavia said. "Do you want me to bring your other clothes in here? Just tell me your locker combination."

Tavia started to rise. Grace reached out and grabbed her arm. Her hand was so cold that Tavia could feel the imprint of each individual bone. "I can still feel him in me."

"Who?" Tavia asked. Grace's grip tightened on Tavia's arm. Tavia didn't pull away. She sat down next to Grace on the cold, damp tiles of the shower floor. "Who?" she repeated.

"Because if I knew what it felt like . . . if I just knew . . ." A shudder ripped through Grace's body.

"You were raped," Tavia said. Because you're gay, she added to herself. It was no big secret. Grace wasn't militant about it. But she wasn't a don't-ask-don't-tell kind of girl either.

"It's still in there. Filth." Grace reached her free hand up toward the cold water tap.

Tavia gently pulled her hand away. "You need to get dry. Then we need to have the principal call the cops and haul the Neanderthal who did this to you away."

Grace finally lifted her head and looked at Tavia. Her gaze turned Tavia's spine to ice. "Not one," Grace said. "Not just one."

"Okay, cover your eyes," Seth told Jane.

"I thought you said no one would be in there," Jane protested.

"Just in case." Jane covered her eyes with one hand. Seth grabbed the other one. Instantly, Jane's fingers twined tightly around his. Just like that. Even after she knew the truth.

Seth opened the side door to the guys' locker room. "Anybody in there?" he called. There was no answer. So he pulled Jane inside. "This is absolutely the best way to sneak back in after you cut," he explained as he led her down a row of lockers.

"It stinks," Jane answered.

"No, it doesn't," Seth said. He pulled in a deep breath. "Okay, yes it does. But I love this smell. It's like the smell of happiness."

"That's so cute," Jane cooed. "The smell of happiness."

That's so dorky, Seth thought. "I guess it's 'cause I'm usually happy when I'm playing basketball," he explained. "Or baseball. Anything. It gets me out of my head."

"Reading is like that for me," Jane told him. "I'll actually read the back of the cereal box if there's nothing else around."

"That's the only thing I do read," Seth joked. "There are some fascinating nutritional facts there. Also, sometimes there's a riddle or even a maze."

Seth opened the door to the gym a crack and peered inside. "All clear. You can open your eyes now." He didn't let go of her hand even though she didn't need him to guide her. She didn't slip her hand away.

"Hard to believe this is where the dance was. It looks so different in the day without all the decorations." She looked up at him, and he felt it again. Every time her gaze met his he felt this, this *zing* that shot from chest to stomach to groin.

"I never got to kiss you." Christ, he'd said it out loud. He hadn't meant to say it out loud. What was it about Jane? When he was around her the sieve between his brain and his mouth opened up and he said any damn thing that came into his head.

"I know," Jane answered. She knew. So she'd noticed. So she'd thought about it. "With the ghosts, and Mr. Williams, and the evil, and the madness . . ." She looked at him again. Massive zing. More like getting hit with those paddles they use to start your heart.

Jane stopped walking. She turned toward him, just a fraction. But it was like she wanted him to kiss her. Right here. Right now. His whole body felt electrified now. He was surprised you couldn't see each nerve glowing through his clothes.

Seth released Jane's hand and wrapped his arms around her waist. She slid her arms around his shoulders. And they looked at each other. The first time I'm gonna kiss someone, Seth thought. At least he didn't say that out loud. It's not like he'd never wanted to. But he'd always thought . . . He'd never thought if someone knew everything about him, what he'd done, she'd even want to be in the same room with him.

His eyes dropped to Jane's lips. They were slightly parted. He could see a tiny flash of pink tongue. Seth lowered his head.

"I never kissed anyone," Jane blurted out before his lips could touch hers. "Oh, my god. I didn't mean to say that.

But it's true. I'm a loser. Who hasn't kissed someone by the time they're fifteen? But just in case I suck at it, you'll know why."

"I never kissed anyone either," Seth admitted. "So if you suck at it, I won't know."

"And I—" Seth didn't let her finish. He couldn't wait another second. He had to taste her. Jane's lips were warm and soft. Could anything really be so soft?

That was the last thought he had, before his whole world became sensation. Jane's heart beating against his chest. Her hands against his face. Her mouth, christ, her mouth.

Closer, closer, he had to get even closer. He flicked his tongue against her lips. Was it okay? Did she want— Her tongue met his, and he heard her make this little sound, almost a purr, from deep in her throat.

Seth moved his hands up and slipped them into her hair. Soft, warm, electric. He—

Jane jerked away. Seth felt as if he'd been thrown into a tub of ice.

"Did you hear that?" she cried.

Before he could answer, he *did* hear it. A scream. Coming from the girls' locker room. Seth and Jane bolted into the locker room and ran toward the sound, Seth's sneakers squeaking when they reached the tiles of the shower room.

His eyes flew immediately to the broken glass of the small window above the last shower. Then to the spray of blood. Seth skidded to a stop in front of the shower stall and looked down. Grace Harding lay in Tavia's lap. A puddle of water and blood surrounded them. "Get the nurse!" Tavia cried.

"I'll go," Jane shouted.

Seth ripped off his shirt and tossed it to Tavia. She wrapped it around Grace's right wrist and pressed down hard. "I'll get towels," Seth told her. Before he could get back with them, Jane and the nurse raced into the locker room. Seth followed them over to Grace.

"What happened?" the nurse demanded.

"She shoved her fist through that window," Tavia answered. Seth saw the muscles of her throat working. "I think she hit a vein."

"There's a stretcher in my office. Go get it," the nurse ordered.

Seth led the way, Tavia and Jane close behind him. "She was raped too. More than one guy. Like a pack of dogs," Tavia told them as soon as they were out of the locker room. "If we don't do something fast, there's not going to be anybody in town left to save."

"I don't know if this will work," Tavia said. She ran one finger down the ginger cat's back.

"Terry said that animals can sense things," Seth told her.

Jane reached down and touched the cat's pink nose. "You can do it, kitty." At least she hoped it could. If they could find the source of the evil—evil, what a small, pathetic word for something so monstrous—they'd have a starting place. Although what they'd do with that starting place, she had no clue.

"All right. Listen to me, pretty cat," Tavia said, looking

into the kitty's yellow eyes. "I want you to take me to the heart of the evil. The center. The source." She glanced over her shoulder at Seth and Jane. "I don't think it's the words they understand. I think it's just thoughts. But it helps me to say it out loud." She turned back to the cat. "Okay, now go!"

All the hair on the ginger cat's body stood up, its tail growing to twice its normal size. It's terrified, Jane realized. But the cat turned around and started to run.

Tavia, Jane, and Seth ran after it. Across lawns. Over fences. The cat wriggled through a rosebush. Tavia and Seth vaulted over. Jane circled it and kept running. Past the DiFranciscos' house. Past the Morgans'. Past the Bluths'.

My neighborhood, she realized. We're in my neighborhood.

The cat rounded the corner. We're on my *street*, Jane thought.

The cat raced across the street and straight toward a white house with blue shutters. Jane's house. Oh, god. Her house.

Without hesitation the cat shot up the trunk of the big maple tree in Jane's front yard, its claws easily digging into the bark. It turned onto one of the long branches and scampered across. Then it began to scratch at one of the windows.

Elijah's window.

Chapter 12

Elijah and Elijah

Tavia reached Elijah's bedroom first. She hesitated outside the closed door. Jane reached around her and shoved it open. The ginger cat was still clawing at the window. Its front paws were bleeding, leaving streaks of red on the glass. Elijah just lay on his back watching it, as if it were a bird sitting in a tree or something.

"No! You're hurting yourself!" Tavia cried. She rushed over to the window and jerked it open. In one soaring leap, the ginger cat was through the window and onto Elijah's bed. It stepped onto Elijah's chest. It curled back its top lip, showing its wicked teeth, and it began to growl, low in its throat, a sound that made Tavia's stomach shrivel.

"Okay, good cat. Thank you," Tavia said in a rush. "You can go now. Go on home." The ginger cat streaked out the door. Part of Tavia wished she could run after it. Elijah. Elijah was the source of the evil. Were they supposed to *kill* him? How could she do that? The answer was, she couldn't. She couldn't.

"Hey, Elijah. Where's Marti?" Jane asked. Her voice

came out loud and overcheerful, like someone talking to a kindergartner.

"She went out a while ago," Elijah answered. "I don't know where."

It was his voice, but it wasn't. It had the same tone and pitch. But there was no . . . no *Elijah* in it.

"Oh. Okay. Well." Jane shifted her weight from foot to foot. "You know what—we're going to go down to the kitchen and get something to eat. Do you want something?"

Elijah shrugged.

"So. Okay. Then we'll choose something for you," Jane answered. "Come on," she said to Tavia and Seth. They followed her to the kitchen in silence and just stood there, staring at one another.

"Crap," Seth finally said.

"Yeah," Tavia agreed.

Jane sank down in one of the chairs as if her legs had been boned. Seth sat down next to her and took her hand. Tavia's hands felt so empty. They had each other. She had no one. Jane looked up at her. Then she reached her free hand out. Tavia took it, sitting on the other side of Jane. And she felt the vibration again, the energy rushing between them. Impulsively, she leaned across the table and grabbed Seth's other hand. The energy doubled. Hot. Pulsing. Charging as it raced through the circle of Tavia, Seth, and Jane.

"We were supposedly given gifts to fight the evil," Seth began.

"But how are seeing ghosts, communicating with animals, and time traveling going to help us?" Tavia asked.

"Well, your animal thing got us here," Seth answered.

Jane spoke for the first time since they entered the kitchen. "We can't hurt Elijah." The energy coursing between them flared. Tavia could almost feel her nerves crackling.

"If he's the source . . . " Seth didn't complete the thought.

Jane stood up, breaking the circle of hands. The energy still flashed between Tavia and Seth, but the heat and intensity died down. Gently, Tavia slipped her hand away from Seth's.

"*He's* not the source," Jane said, starting to pace around the table. "The source is *in* him."

Seth opened his mouth, as if he wanted to say something, then shut it. Smart boy, Tavia thought. "I agree with Jane," she told Seth. "I was with Elijah, the real Elijah. It was like he was free of the evil for a few moments, and I talked to him. To *him*."

"Yes!" Jane exclaimed. "He quacked at me. That was the real Elijah."

"What?" Tavia asked.

"Never mind. Doesn't matter," Jane answered. "But it was like you said—the real, true Elijah was out. He was with me."

Seth tapped his fingers on the table. Tavia wondered if his hands were getting those sharp little pains that hers were, the pains you got when your hands had fallen asleep and then you started to move them again. "I guess the first step of whatever our plan is has to be separating

Elijah from the evil."

"Right," Tavia jumped in. "We can't fight the evil if it's inside Elijah. We could end up killing him."

"That's not going to happen," Jane said. "It can't. My parents just got Elijah back. If they lost him again . . . "

"You both said you've had moments with the real Elijah," Seth commented. "Do you think you can, I don't know, bring him out? If you could talk to him, maybe he could help us get the thing out into the open."

Tavia looked over at Jane. "We could try it," Jane said.

"We should definitely try it," Tavia agreed.

Seth didn't reply. Tavia glanced at him. His eyes were locked on the kitchen window. "What do you see?" Tavia asked him.

"Ghosts. A whole lot of ghosts in the front yard." Seth stood up. "I need to talk to them."

"We'll go upstairs and work on Elijah," Jane said. "Be careful."

"You too," Seth answered. A look of such intensity passed between them that Tavia had to lower her head. That's what it looks like. The real deal. Love, she thought. You never would have had that with Thomas, no matter how sweet he was before . . . before it got him. The madness. The evil.

"Ready?" Jane asked.

"As I'll ever be," Tavia answered. She and Jane retraced their steps up to Elijah's room.

"We forgot to bring snacks. Sorry," Jane told her brother. She sat down on the edge of his bed. Tavia could see the tension in her back and shoulders. She felt it in her own body when she sat down on the other side of Elijah. They were so close, so close to the thing that was destroying their town.

"Remember those sandwiches you used to make?" Jane continued. "Graham crackers and mustard on white bread."

Elijah gave a little grunt in reply. Jane jerked her chin toward Tavia. My turn, Tavia thought. "Remember when you painted my name on the roof of the gym—and I got in trouble for it?"

No response. Not even a grunt this time. And his eyes were shuttered. If there was any Elijah peering through, Tavia couldn't see it.

"Remember the stories Dad used to tell us about the mice who lived behind the refrigerator?" Jane asked. "Squeaky and Silver?"

"Remember that candy necklace I gave you? It got to be our way of apologizing—giving each other necklaces," Tavia asked. "You actually wore it until it melted in all those colored streaks down your chest." And I licked them off, she added silently. She didn't want to say that in front of Jane. Except maybe that's exactly the kind of thing that would pull Elijah to her.

"I licked the sugar smears off you, remember?" Tavia added, feeling heat surge into her cheeks. "You picked a fight with me the next day, just so you could give me an apology necklace that would melt all over me."

Had that gotten a flicker of response? Tavia wasn't sure.

"Remember when you cut your ankle on the sprinkler head that time we were playing hide-and-seek with everyone in the neighborhood?" Jane asked. "Remember how when I was little I started laughing as soon as I hid. I couldn't stand waiting in the dark for someone to find me."

"Remember how Mr. Gelson put us on the opposite sides of that debate in history class, just because he knew we were going out? Remember how he liked to play god like that?" Tavia asked.

Remember, remember, remember. Tavia and Jane threw out memories like lifelines. But Elijah just stared up at the ceiling, mouth slack.

He's worse than he was when we first came in here, Tavia thought. Should we stop?

No, they couldn't. They couldn't give up. They just needed to try something different. "Jane, do you think I could be alone with Elijah for a little while?"

"Are you sure you want to?" Jane's hazel eyes were dark with concern.

Tavia nodded. Jane slowly stood, then left the room, shutting the door softly behind her.

Memory isn't just about words, Tavia thought. It's scents, tastes, sensations. She grabbed her purse and pulled out the roll of cinnamon LifeSavers. She broke one of the LifeSavers in half—she didn't want Elijah to choke—and gently slid it between his parted lips.

"Remember?" she whispered. Then she leaned down and covered his slack mouth with her own. He has to remember this, he has to, she thought as she kissed him, try-ing to transfer strength and courage and, yes, *love* to him. She didn't want to love him. Love got in the way of your plans. Love hurt so bad you felt as if someone were killing you every single day. But she couldn't help it. She loved him.

Elijah's lips grew eager under hers. And he was with her, kissing her. She'd try to talk to him in a minute, in just one minute, but she couldn't pull away, not yet.

Tavia stretched out her body against Elijah's. He brought his hands up to her throat, stroking.

Squeezing.

Choking.

Red worms squiggled in front of Tavia's eyes. Blood vessels? Was she seeing her own blood vessels? The worms burst. Tavia's world went red.

Then black.

Vicki Callison slid the IV needle out of her arm. She couldn't stay in the hospital a second longer. Not when Andrea was out there having fun, wearing her little outfits, showing off her flat belly, showing off her hands with their perfect manicure.

She didn't have a flat belly. Not anymore, thanks to Andrea. She didn't have a perfect manicure. How could she? Half her fingers were gone. Thanks to Andrea.

Vicki was getting her life back. And that meant Andrea was losing hers. Today.

Thomas studied the skin of his arm. It wasn't white. The sheet on his hospital bed was white. His skin was red and gooey yellow. Not white.

He pinched a piece of skin between two fingers and tugged. Tears flooded his eyes, but he kept pulling until he'd torn away a long strip of the not-white skin. Maybe when it grew back it would be the right color. For Tavia.

Thomas wiped his bloody fingers on his hospital gown. Then he pinched another piece of skin.

"Stupid, baby Lily," JoJo Johansson muttered. "Got me in trouble."

She snuck out of her room and tiptoed into the kitchen, holding a Barbie in each hand. Then she did what she was never, ever supposed to do—she turned one of the stove knobs.

The front burner gave a whoosh and blue flames appeared. JoJo stuck one of the Barbie's heads into the blaze. Its face melted right off. Good. That's what she thought would happen. That's what she was going to do to stupid, stinky, baby Lily.

"He called me a— I can't repeat it, but it was nasty," Marti Neemy said, making sure to get her lower lip trembling.

"That is so wrong," the lowlife answered. "Want me to talk to him for you?"

Marti wrinkled up her nose. "Talk?"

The lowlife curled his hands into fists and held them up. "Talk with these," he said.

Marti smiled and handed him a knife. "He'll hear better if you use this."

"So that's it? That's all you got?" Seth asked.

"Yep," Terry answered. "Like I said, I kept telling them about how there were three of you and you were looking for the fourth and how you had to find the source of the evil, and they finally seemed to get it, and they brought me here."

The other ghosts, the ones who had chased Seth up to the point, including his buddy, the blood-dripping naked guy; the kid with the noose; and the four blazing kids—stood in a semicircle on Jane's lawn, staring up at Elijah's window, speechless, expressionless.

Terry ran his hands through his shaggy brown hair. "Sucks that it turned out to be your girlfriend's brother."

"She's not my—" Seth stopped himself. Maybe Jane wasn't his girlfriend . . . yet. But he wanted her to be. "Thanks for kicking my butt and getting me to call her."

Terry grinned. "I know you kissed her. About time. There's no reason for us both to die virgins." Terry punched Seth's arm, and his fist sank into Seth's flesh. Cold radiated out from Terry's fist in widening circles.

Terry pulled back his hand. He flexed his fingers. And Seth could see his bones. "What the—" Seth raised his eyes. The skin of Terry's face was thinning, the color fading until Terry's skull was visible. "What's happening?"

"I guess I'm done here," Terry answered. Clumps of his brown hair lightened until they were translucent, then they fell out and flew away in the breeze. "I thought I'd be able to stay with you until after, after whatever's going to happen, but—" His shoulder bones rose up and down in a shrug.

"Done? With what?" Seth tried not to stare as Terry's eyes lightened from brown to tan to white. Even his pupils went white.

"You were the only reason I was hanging around,"

Terry answered. "You were just so danged tortured." He shook his head, the bones of his neck looking too fragile to support his skull.

"Shouldn't that have made you happy?" Seth couldn't help asking.

"Oh, it was fun for a while," Terry admitted. His eyes were clear now. Seth could see straight through to the sky. "When I was still pissed at you. But all that crap burned away pretty fast. Once you're dead, all that really stays with you is what you love." He gave a loud fake sniffle. "And I love you, dude." His voice grew thin. "I wanted you to be okay. And I guess you are. Or I wouldn't be going."

"Yeah, I am, because of you," Seth answered. Terry's bones began to glow, turning the world pure white.

When the brilliance faded, Terry was gone. So were the other ghosts.

"I love you too, dude," he added softly, hoping his best friend had heard. Doesn't matter if he didn't, Seth thought. He knows.

Matthew Plett was sick of this Russian roulette bull-crap. His father had been too freakin' lucky. If his dad had made one game, one freakin' game, maybe he'd deserve some luck.

But he didn't. So he didn't.

Matthew got a plastic funnel out from under the sink. He pulled out the bottle of Liquid Plumr. He'd pour it straight down the old man's throat.

* * *

Muffin ate a piece of dog food. Hard, dry, flavorless. The garage door was open a little way. Muffin squeezed underneath it. She sniffed. There was better food out here. Tender, juicy, rich. Flesh, that's what she wanted. More human flesh.

Charlie Williams loaded the rifle. He was the dad. He would deal with it. And the only way to deal with it was to kill them. The only way to keep his family from the sax and violins and evil of the world was to kill them. Then he'd kill himself. And they'd all be together. In a safe place. In a better place.

Jane paced in front of Elijah's door. She didn't hear anything. Not that she was trying to hear actual words. She wanted to give Tavia and Elijah privacy for . . . whatever Tavia wanted it for. But shouldn't she be able to hear *something*? She hesitated. Touched the doorknob. Pulled her hand back.

"How's it going?"

She turned and saw Seth heading up the stairs. Looking at him, it was like swallowing a little piece of the sun, even in the middle of all this madness, this darkness, coldness.

"I don't know," Jane admitted. "Tavia wanted some time alone with Elijah. It hasn't been that long, but to be honest, I'm getting a little nervous."

Seth strode up to the door and knocked. No answer.

"Tavia?" Jane called. No answer. She threw the door open. Elijah lay on his bed, staring at the ceiling, just as he had been when she'd left the room.

But Tavia? Where was Tavia?

Jane's breath left her lungs with a whoosh. Tavia was lying on the floor. Still. So still. Jane rushed to Tavia's side and dropped to her knees. Pulse. That was the first thing to do, check for a pulse. She rested her fingertips on Tavia's throat and felt a heavy thudding. But it was coming from inside Jane's own body. Her heart was beating so hard she could feel it all over—in her fingertips, her wrists, her chest, of course, but also in her earlobes, and in the flesh of one corner of her lower lip. Thud, thud, thud.

Thud!

That wasn't her heart. Jane whipped her head toward the sound . . . and saw Elijah slam Seth's head into the wall. Thud! Seth wrapped his long fingers around Elijah's neck and squeezed. Elijah's face darkened to an angry purple, but he managed to ram Seth's skull into the wall again. Seth's hands slithered away from Elijah's neck. Was he unconscious? Dead?

"It's me you want!" Jane screamed so loud she could almost feel her vocal cords fraying. "I let myself burn last time to kill you, and I'll do it again."

Elijah released Seth, and Seth slid down the wall to the floor, body limp. "I'll do it," Jane shouted again. "I'll go get the other three and we'll do it right now." She didn't know if Elijah—not Elijah, not her brother, the *evil*, could sense that Tavia, and Seth were two of the three. All she could do was pray it didn't.

I've got to get the evil away from them, she thought. She turned her back on Seth and Tavia and started for the door. An instant later, she heard Elijah's footsteps coming toward her. And she felt a shift in her brain. Slowly, she turned and looked behind her.

Elijah sat on the floor, painting a papier-mâché ball the blue and white of the Earth. For the mobile, Jane thought. Sixth grade. I got sent back. Elijah's in the sixth grade. He's twelve.

But where was the other Elijah, the one the evil was using? Was it still in the present? Had it returned to bashing Seth's brains out?

Elijah looked up, and the paintbrush slipped from his fingers. He sees me, Jane thought. He hadn't before. Only her younger self and her past life self had been able to see her the other times.

"Who are you?" Elijah asked, his voice calm and curious.

"I'm—" Jane began.

"I'm you," someone answered from behind her. She turned. Elijah, seventeen-year-old Elijah, stood there. "Don't worry. I just came to get something. I'll be gone in a second."

Elijah—the evil—stepped toward Jane. It's going to kill me now. The knowledge was like a hammer blow to the temple. She felt dazed, unable to move, unable to think.

"You're not me," twelve-year-old Elijah answered.

"I will be," the Elijah thing told him.

"You're not me," the young Elijah insisted. He hurled himself at the Elijah thing.

"Don't!" Jane cried. She reached for the young Elijah, but her fingers passed right through him. He slammed into the evil Elijah and they merged.

A howl erupted from Elijah's mouth, a howl that sounded

as if it originated in hell. Elijah's arms and legs began to spasm. One leg shrank until it was so much shorter than the other that he toppled.

Jane's stomach cramped as she stared at him sprawled on the floor. Stare was all she could do. She was powerless here. She stared as an eye appeared in Elijah's forehead, then was reabsorbed. She stared as his hands collapsed on themselves, then sprang back out to their original size with a horrible cracking sound.

They're fighting for control in there, Jane realized. Two bodies, two beings, twisted together, battling.

Shudder after shudder ripped through Elijah—the melded Elijahs. Then the body, their body, stiffened and went still. An oily yellow-green liquid began to leak from his—their— mouth and ears and eyes.

It's dead, Jane thought. The evil is dead.

And so was her brother.

Elijah past, Elijah present, they were both dead.

I did not think I would have the strength to change forms again so soon. But I have found a host who cannot resist me. I was brought right to him because it was thought I might help him heal. How fortunate.

Inside, I am able to draw out the food I need from everyone who comes near. Well, almost everyone. There are a few, a very few, who manage to block me. But most are ripe, so ripe I hardly need to do anything. So much hate. So much love ready to plunge into hate. So much envy. So much greed. So much fear. So much food. I want it all. I must not destroy the two that provide shelter and food for this form. I could not resist tasting them, but I did not do more than taste. They are needed to keep this body alive until I no longer have any use for it.

There is plenty of other food. And as I feed, my power will double, and double again. Then I will have no need for a host. I will be free. And my enemies will burn.

Chapter 13

The Fourth

Charlie Williams dropped the rifle.

JoJo Johansson dropped the Barbie and turned off the stove.

Vicki Callison dropped the little circular saw, the one she'd planned to use to cut off her daughter's head.

Matthew Plett dropped the funnel and the Liquid Plumr, and left the house, his fat-butt father safe and sound in front of the tube.

Muffin stopped thinking about food, flesh food, and trotted toward the center of town, tail wagging.

Marti Neemy wandered out of the bar. The lowlife dropped the knife she'd given him.

Thomas Bledsoe stopped peeling the skin from his body.

He shoved himself out of bed and stood on the cool linoleum floor, blood dripping from his wounds.

Tavia opened her eyes. Elijah leaned over her. She recoiled.

Elijah held up both hands, palms forward, the universal symbol for "I'm unarmed. I'm not going to hurt you." "It's me, Tavie," he told her. "It's me."

"It is," Jane added. Tavia turned her head and saw Jane with her arm around Seth's waist, half supporting his weight. "I don't know how it happened exactly. We both went back in time, to when we were kids. And it was like the younger Elijah knew there was something wrong with the older one."

"He ran right into me," Elijah burst out. "I could feel him—me, that me—inside with us." He swallowed hard. "Us. Me and . . . " He squeezed his eyes shut.

Tavia reached out and touched fingertips with Elijah. He curled his fingers around hers, as if he were drawing strength from her, then opened his eyes and continued. "I don't know how he, the little me, did it, but I felt the evil start to leak out of me."

"And I saw it," Jane jumped in. "It came out of his eyes and his ears and his mouth. I thought he was dead. I thought you both might be dead too," she told Seth and Tavia.

"I have a hard head," Seth told her.

"Still," Jane said, "I think I should clean out those gashes. Come on." She led him to the door, then looked back at Elijah. "I missed you."

"I missed you too, Quane," Elijah answered. "Now get out of my room so I can be alone with my girlfriend."

"Girlfriend." The word knocked the breath out of Tavia. You love him, you know that, so what's your problem? she asked herself as Jane and Seth left the room and closed the door behind them.

Elijah released her hand. "Sorry. I guess I shouldn't have used the *G* word."

"So do you remember . . . everything?" Tavia asked. Like what I told you about me and Thomas, she silently added.

"The first thing I remember is waking up and feeling strong and hyper alert, like they'd been feeding me steroids and amphetamines through the IV," Elijah answered. "It was a complete rush. Everything was amazing to me—the feel of the sheets, the colors in the quilt on my bed, the smell of antiseptic, even the feel of saliva going down my throat and air moving in and out of my lungs."

Elijah's voice sped up as he talked, like he was experiencing the exhilaration again. Tavia couldn't keep her eyes off his face, so animated, so alive. As she watched, the pleasure drained away.

"Then I realized I couldn't move. No, I *was* moving, but I wasn't controlling the movements myself," Elijah continued. "And, you know, I didn't know why I was in the hospital. Or why Jane looked so different."

"You must have been terrified," Tavia said.

"I should have been, but a lot of the time it was like I was drugged. Everything seemed muted. And I really didn't care." Elijah rubbed his face with his fingers. "I had to battle against that. But I don't think fighting is what did it. Sometimes I think it—the evil's—attention was on something else, and I could surface."

"Why didn't you tell anyone?" Tavia asked.

"I never remembered. Until I was back under." A shudder rippled through Elijah's body.

And she had to touch him, had to. She reached out and ran her fingers down his cheek.

Elijah reached out and covered her hand with his, keeping her fingers pressed against his face. "So, does this mean . . . I heard what you said to me about Thomas. But I also felt you kissing me, and it felt like, well, not like a friend kiss."

Tavia slid her hand out from under Elijah's. "Thomas—" She stopped herself. Now wasn't the time to tell Elijah that Thomas was in the hospital and why. "I was going out with Thomas, but I never felt about him the way I feel about you. And, really, that was the thing that I liked most about him."

"I don't get it," Elijah said. His eyes darted back and forth, just fractions each way, like they always did when he was listening with full-on intensity. Nobody could listen like Elijah.

"He was safe," Tavia answered.

"And I'm not safe? I'm Mr. Safe. I was even school safety monitor," Elijah protested, his tone teasing but his expression serious.

"I don't want to love anybody, not now, and Thomas was safe because I knew, deep down, that I'd never even get close," Tavia admitted.

"Not now," Elijah repeated. "You mean because of

college and law school and getting an internship."

Tavia nodded. He still knows me so well, she thought.

"But since you didn't feel about Thomas the way you feel about me— That's what you said, right, feel, present tense?" He didn't pause for an answer. "Since you didn't feel about Thomas the way you feel about me, and you didn't come close to loving Thomas, it means you love me. Not just that you did. But that you do."

Elijah's eyes started doing the back-and-forth thing again as he looked at her, waiting for a response. She wanted to say yes. She wanted to say no. So she ended up not saying anything.

"You do," Elijah said again. He cupped her face in his hands and lowered his head. Tavia's heart kicked in her chest. He was going to kiss her.

"I don't want to," she blurted out.

"Why?" Elijah asked, his mouth so close to hers that she could feel his warm breath on her lips.

"Because, because I almost died myself when you went into the coma. I don't want to love anybody so much that it'll kill me," Tavia told him without pulling away.

"I do," Elijah said. "That's exactly how much I want to love someone."

There was a long beat of silence as they looked into each other's eyes. She didn't ever want to be hurt the way she had been when she lost Elijah. But did she really want to go through the rest of her life only feeling things on the surface?

No. The answer was so strong it rocked her whole body.

And she kissed Elijah, kissed him until he was her whole world. And for the first time in almost two years, she felt truly alive.

Tavia heard Elijah give a little moan. Then she heard a cracking sound, and Elijah's lips slid off hers. She opened her eyes.

Elijah's jawbones gave another crack as they stretched open. Farther, farther. Tavia stumbled away from him, her eyes locked on his mouth. There was something moving in there.

A thick snakelike roll of yellow-green slime shoved its way out of Elijah's mouth. It wove from side to side, graceful, horrible.

"E-Elijah," Tavia stammered. She forced herself to look into Elijah's eyes—that's the only thing that would save her sanity. They were wide and bright with terror. Could he even see her?

The snake of slime wove closer, brushing against Tavia's cheek. The wet, spongy feel of the thing sent a scream clawing up her throat. Don't open your mouth, not with that thing so close, she ordered herself. But the scream kept coming.

"You're the hero," Jane told Seth. She kissed him on the tip of the ear.

"No, you're the hero," he answered. He kissed her on the throat, right in that little hollow at the base.

"You're the—"

Jane was interrupted by a long, shrill scream. The sound made Seth feel as if someone had gutted him with a cold knife.

"Tavia!" Jane cried. She threw open the bathroom door.

Something snaked down the hall. Yellow-green. And fast. Getting bigger as it moved. It was gone before Seth could get a good look at it, leaving behind a thick trail of glistening mucus. A second later, Tavia and Elijah burst out of Elijah's bedroom. "That thing crawled right out of his mouth," Tavia cried.

"I didn't know it was still in there." Elijah scrubbed his mouth with the back of its hand. "It faked me out. It let me think I was in control, and then . . . "

"We've got to go after it." Jane's face was pale, but her voice came out strong and steady. "We've got to end this."

"We can't just chase it down," Tavia protested. "We need a plan."

"How can we come up with a plan until we know more about it?" Seth asked. "We have no idea how to kill the thing." He turned to Elijah. "Did you pick up anything when it was, you know, inside you? Anything we can use?"

"It wasn't a sharing, communicating, touchy-feely kind of evil," Elijah answered. He sounded a little pissed, not that Seth blamed him.

"We have to at least see what it's doing out there," Jane insisted. She didn't wait for an answer. She followed the trail down the hall and disappeared around the corner.

Seth wasn't letting Jane go after the thing herself, that was for damn sure. He caught up to her, Tavia and Elijah right behind him. They rushed downstairs. The mucus continued across the living room carpet, matting down the fibers and staining them that sickening yellow green.

"That sucker is fast," Elijah muttered as they followed

the trail out the door. The streak of mucus went down the walkway to the sidewalk, and down the sidewalk to the end of the block, where it turned the corner and disappeared.

"Let's take my car." Seth pulled out his keys and ran over to the Volvo. His mom always insisted he drive it to school when it was cold. He slid in the driver's seat, and they were off. He pushed the gas pedal down until they were doing ninety, but they didn't catch up to the thing.

"It's heading to the path up to the point," Tavia cried.

Seth gripped the wheel so hard his hands ached. He took the corner without braking, the Volvo's tires squealing. "We'll have to get out here." He forced himself to bring the car to a slow, controlled stop.

An instant later he was out of the car, running up the path, Jane, Elijah, and Tavia beside him. Just before they reached the top, Jane grabbed his arm with both hands and pulled him to a stop. "Look."

He stood there with the others, panting, trying to absorb what he was seeing.

A—a tree, or something like a tree, a small yellow-green tree with thin, undulating, snakelike branches—had sprouted in the clearing at the top of the point.

"What do you think? Fire?" Elijah asked, breaking the silence. "Or just chop the mother down?"

"We don't know anything about its physiology," Tavia answered. "What if it feeds on fire? What if it can regenerate? We could end up making it stronger."

"We can't just sit here," Jane protested.

Seth heard footsteps behind him. "Crap." He jerked his head toward the sound. "Mr. Williams," he shouted. "Get back." He searched for something sane sounding. "That thing is poisonous." Mr. Williams kept walking toward the tree, not even glancing in Seth's direction.

Seth sprinted toward Mr. Williams. He couldn't let Chad's dad get close to that thing. It would kill him. Seth was sure of that. "Get back!" he shouted again.

This time Mr. Williams seemed to hear Seth. He turned toward him and opened his mouth to answer. Fast as a snake striking, one of the writhing tree branches shot into Mr. Williams's open mouth.

Seth kept running, making sure to keep his jaws locked together. He slid to a stop in front of Mr. Williams. He wasn't dead. His eyes were wide and blank, unblinking. His face expressionless. But Seth could see Mr. Williams's pulse beating in the base of his throat. It, the evil, hadn't killed him. Yet.

A shudder ripped through Seth's body as one of the branches, whatever they were, probed the back of his neck, leaving a streak of mucus. He pressed his teeth together until he thought they'd crack off, but the branch weaved away without trying to penetrate his mouth.

"Oh, god, Mr. Williams," Jane cried as she ran up to Seth, Tavia and Elijah at her side. She stepped up and ran her fingers down Mr. Williams's face. "It's me. Jane. Can you hear me?" Mr. Williams's expression didn't change. He didn't even twitch.

"I don't think you should be touching him," Elijah said. He reached for his sister. Jane shrugged out of his grasp.

"Do you hear that?" she whispered.

Seth listened. But the only thing he heard was his heartbeat thundering in his ears. He shook his head.

"It's coming from the vine thing," Jane said. Seth moved closer to the thin, weaving branch that ran from Mr. Williams's mouth to the tree. He did hear something—a hissing, whispering sound. He moved even closer, fighting his revulsion as he brought his ear down to the branch.

"I'm the dad, I have to deal with it. All the sax and violins. Better dead. Chad, Beth, Alexis—all better dead. In a better place. Better dead."

Seth raised his head, feeling as if he'd just taken a long swig of battery acid. "You heard it, didn't you?" Jane asked. "It's like . . . didn't you think it was almost like you were hearing Mr. Williams's thoughts?" she continued.

"Incoming," Elijah called out. He pointed down the hill. Seth saw one of the little girls who'd been throwing rocks at the school. And he was pretty sure Andrea Callison's mother.

"Thomas," Tavia whispered. Seth followed her gaze to a boy, he guessed it was a boy, trailing behind the little girl and Mrs. Callison. Could that really be Thomas Bledsoe? It could, Seth decided. Could be anyone. Its—his, Seth corrected himself—face looked like it was made of raw hamburger. Hot bile splashed into Seth's throat and he forced himself to swallow it. That's all you saw when you looked at Thomas. Blood. Flesh. With two dark eyes peering out.

As Seth watched, one of the yellow-green branches shot toward Thomas and dove into the bloody hole that was Thomas's mouth. How could one of the branches reach that far? Thomas hadn't even passed Seth yet.

Seth whipped his head toward the tree. His heart slammed against his ribs, as if it wanted to break out of his chest and run away. The tree had doubled in size. They'd been out here what, five minutes, and it had *doubled* in size.

"I hear Thomas," Tavia said. Her voice sounded thick, choked with unshed tears.

Seth leaned close to the branch—more like an umbilical cord—that connected Thomas to the tree.

"She wants a white boy, I'll give her one. I'll rip my skin off and grow a new one for the bitch. Not good enough for her this way. Wants a white boy. Fine."

He's thinking about Tavia, Seth realized. He shot a glance at her. Should he say something? Would that just make it worse?

"I think it's feeding on these people," Elijah said. "That's how it's growing so fast."

Tavia grabbed the branch connecting Thomas to the tree and gave it a vicious yank. Thomas let out an animal howl that made Seth's balls try to crawl back inside him.

Elijah pried Tavia's fingers off the branch. The howling turned to a whimper.

"We hurt the tree, we hurt them—is that right?" Jane asked.

"Looks like it," Seth answered.

"And there are more coming," Elijah announced. "That's Marti, my nurse."

"Get the hell away from here," Seth shouted to her. But Marti kept coming. She placidly opened her mouth and allowed the squirming branch inside.

"All these people have been around me since I came out

of the hospital," Elijah said. "Marti, obviously. And Mr. Williams was over all the time."

"Mrs. Callison was in your room when you woke up," Jane added. "And the little girl, JoJo, she was one of the Brownies who made you that banner, wasn't she?"

Elijah nodded. "The evil, it primed them somehow."

"Maybe that's why we aren't sucking on those branches right now," Seth said. "Maybe you have to be, like you said, primed first."

"You know how many people I've been in contact with since I did my miracle wake up?" Elijah asked. "Half the town, at least. I don't know if it got to them all, but—"

"Incoming," Tavia called out.

Yeah, here came Matthew Plett. Seth really didn't want to hear the sewage that would come out of him.

"Oh, god. My parents," Jane cried.

"I did this to them," Elijah said.

"Don't say that!" Jane gave her brother a little shake. "It wasn't you. It was *that*." She pointed to the tree. It towered over the tallest tree on the point now, its branches like a nest of giant snakes twining, weaving, gracefully waving this way and that.

"It's like they're batteries. Each person pumps more juice into the freakin' tree or whatever it is." Seth couldn't take his eyes off the branches. How many more would grow with this new batch of human batteries?

"It's sucking out the worst in them," Tavia said. "That little girl, she's so full of hate for someone called Lily, another little girl, I think."

"Yeah. She almost killed a little girl named Lily on the

playground. She got a bunch of kids to throw rocks at her," Jane explained.

"And Thomas. He hates himself so much, and it's using that." Tavia's lips curled in revulsion.

"Everything burns away. Except what you love," Seth muttered.

"What?" Jane asked.

"Something Terry told me. All the bull burns away once you're dead. All that's left is what you loved when you were alive," Seth told her.

"Love and hate. Maybe they're like acid and base. Maybe they neutralize each other," Tavia said.

"So we're supposed to love that thing to death?" Elijah burst out. "Somebody get me a puke bucket."

"I got the ghost gift for a reason," Seth answered. "And they're hanging around the island for a reason. I've got to get to the cemetery. I'll be back as fast as I can."

"Okay, for viewers who tuned in late, you all got gifts," Elijah said. "And there's somebody else out there somewhere, the fourth, who is supposed to be helping you in the evil smackdown, but whoever it is hasn't showed. Is that right?"

"That's it," Tavia told him. One of the cords slithered past her foot. She forced herself to keep still. Clearly, they aren't going after us, she told herself.

"It's even using animals," Jane said. She jerked her chin to the left, and Tavia saw a fluffy white-and-tan mutt with a cord connecting it to the tree. "That's Muffin. She was Elijah's therapy dog."

"If it can use animals as power, maybe they can help us too." Tavia felt a little silly, so she closed her eyes and tried to concentrate. *Animals of Raven's Point, I need you*, she thought. *Come to me. Birds, cats, dogs, possums, raccoons, skunks, deer. Every creature of Raven's Point, come to me.* She flashed on the goldfish leaping out of the pond in her yard. *Except fish*, she added quickly. *If it will kill you to come, don't come.*

She opened her eyes, and saw that they were already on their way to her. The sky was dark with birds. The ground trembled with the motion of hundreds of paws and hoofs.

"You did that?" Elijah asked. "Christ, it's like an eclipse." He didn't seem to be able to take his eyes off the sky. The birds had created a new level of atmosphere, blocking out most of the sunlight, filling the air with the heat of their bodies and their thick, powdery smell.

"And an earthquake," Jane added. She grabbed Tavia's arm, and Tavia realized the ground was shaking now as the animals charged closer, sending shockwaves through her body.

Then the earth went still. The animals had come as close to her as they could get, then stopped. Now they stood as motionless as statues. The birds circled overhead, flapping endlessly.

"I don't know what to tell them to do," Tavia cried over the flapping of the thousands of wings, looking from Jane to Elijah.

"So many of them," Jane whispered, awestruck. "You never really think about how many animals you share the world with."

She gave her head a sharp shake, then turned her full attention to Tavia. "You said you thought maybe we could get some neutralizing action going. Can they, I don't know, pump innocence into the tree? The way the others are injecting hate and fear and other nastiness?"

"I don't know how to tell them that. Partly because I don't have any idea how they're actually supposed to do it. But I'll try." Tavia scanned the animals around her. Her eyes lit on a fawn, who was staring right back at her. Tavia didn't bother with words. She filled her mind with an image of the little deer glowing with a pale yellow light, pale but strong. Innocence. Then she pictured the deer's innocence flowing into the tree and the tree beginning to wither.

The fawn ran to the closest tree cord and grabbed it in its teeth. Tavia could see light running through the cord, running back to the heart of the tree. Maybe this could work. Maybe this was all it would take.

But the fawn began to spasm. Foam exploded from its mouth. It fell to the ground, ears, legs, and tail twitching, eyes bulging. Then it went still. Horribly still.

"What was I thinking?" Tavia cried. She felt hot tears begin to flow down her cheeks. She furiously wiped them away. Tears weren't going to bring the fawn back to life. "I'm the one who came up with the brilliant theory that it was like acid and base. How could I have expected one little animal to neutralize all that?"

"Maybe if all the animals went in at one time," Jane began.

"No. No, they could all die. I'm not going to tell them to do that," Tavia answered.

"Uh, guys," Elijah said, his voice shaking. "I've got something happening here."

He held out his palm, and Tavia saw a lavender thread push its way out of Elijah's flesh. It hung in the air like a filament from a spider's web.

"Is it more of the evil? Is there still more in you?" Jane asked. But she didn't sound frightened. And, strangely, Tavia didn't feel frightened.

"I don't think so. I should be freaking seeing this come out of me, but I'm not, not bad freaking anyway," Elijah answered.

"It's actually beautiful," Tavia said, feeling a deep peacefulness fill her as she stared at the thin lavender thread. But could she trust the feeling? Or was it some kind of trick?

Twisting delicately, the thread moved down to a porcupine sitting near Tavia's feet. The porcupine opened its mouth. Before Tavia could order the porcupine away, the thread slipped inside it.

Tavia stared at it, searching for any signs of pain. The animal seemed to feel the same peace she had when she looked at the thread. As she watched, the thread thickened to ribbon, then to cord.

"It's powering *me*," Elijah exclaimed. "The thread. The porcupine. I can feel it."

"I guess we can stop wondering who the fourth is," Jane said, staring at her brother as hundreds of the lavender threads began to sprout from his body, pushing through his hair, his clothes.

Feed him. Fuel him, Tavia silently commanded the

animals. The birds swooped down, then returned to the sky, each connected to Elijah by a section of living lavender thread, thread that rapidly thickened once the attachment was made. They would have lifted him into the sky with them if the ground animals—the cats and dogs and other four footers—hadn't connected themselves to Elijah too.

"Look!" Jane pointed into the swirling mass of birds. Tavia's breath caught in her throat as she saw a single white raven in the mix, its powerful wings stretched wide, a piece of lavender cord disappearing past its sharp beak.

Tavia returned her gaze to the ground. She couldn't see Elijah anymore, only the twisting tapestry of lavender. But the yellow-green cords of the tree were so much thicker.

"It's not enough. Elijah's still not strong enough to fight it. He needs more than the animals." Without thinking, Tavia opened her mouth and invited one of the lavender threads inside her.

And she was with Elijah. She was inside him. Flowing through him. Tasting him. Tasting his love for her. His love for *everything*. It was as if his time in the coma had made him more sensitive to the world, to all its beauty.

Tavia added her love to the mixture. Her love of the feel of grass under her feet. The challenge of taking the point. Her parents. *NSYNC. And Elijah. Her overwhelming, overpowering, never-ending, till-death-do-us-part love of Elijah.

A gasp escaped Jane as she watched the creature that was Elijah and Tavia and the animals grow. She could hardly stand to look at it. It was not beautiful; it was awe inspiring, like a glimpse of eternity, something no mortal should be able to see.

She caught a whiff of something rotten. Smoke. The vines of the tree had started to smoke. And here and there the oily mucus covering the vines caught fire.

Maybe it's over. Maybe it's dying, Jane thought. But the flames weren't consuming the vines. They were becoming part of the vines, twisting around them like caressing hands.

A spark from one of the little fires leapt onto one of the lavender cords. The cord shriveled. And Jane heard a cat give a hiss of pain.

The creature made of Elijah, Tavia, and the animals was awe inspiring. But it wasn't strong enough to survive the evil. Not yet.

I could join it. The thought was tempting. Jane could imagine how wonderful it would feel to join that marvelous being. The peace she would feel. But she couldn't. Not yet. She had to find a way to give it more power.

My time shifts, she thought. I have to be able to use them for something. That was the point of the gifts—to fight the evil. But how?

Jane followed the closest yellow-green vine to its power source—Mr. Williams. She reached out and took his limp hand in hers. She had no idea if this would work, but she had to try *something*. Take us someplace happy, she thought.

The oily smoke that had been filling her lungs and burning her eyes was replaced by clean, fresh air, salty from the ocean. Mr. Williams was down on the beach below the point using that ocean breeze to fly a kite. Alexis, probably age two, was riding piggyback. Chad was rolling in the sand, trying to get away from his mother's tickling fingers.

And they were back. Mr. Williams fell to the ground. The vine pulled free from his mouth and turned to ash. Please don't let that have killed him, Jane thought. She leaned down. He was still breathing, thank god, but unconscious.

Jane moved on to Mrs. Callison. She'd just keep disconnecting the power sources and see what happened. Maybe the tree already had sucked in enough fuel to ultimately burn through the delicate tangle of lavender cords. But all she could do was keep going.

She took Mrs. Callison by the hand and they went back. Jane wasn't sure how many years, but she figured about eighteen if she was right and that bump in Mrs. Callison was the beginning of Andrea.

Mrs. Callison lowered herself slowly to a picnic blanket. She placed both hands on her belly and started to sing to it. "Hush, little baby, don't say a word . . . "

And they were back. Mrs. Callison fell to the ground, free of her connection to the evil. Jane studied the tree. The vine that had been in Mrs. Callison's mouth had crumbled to ash, but otherwise the tree looked as strong as ever. At least it's not getting any more from her, Jane thought.

She moved on to Muffin and dug her fingers into the dog's soft fur. And she was with Muffin, lying under a blackberry bush on the point, nursing from his mother. Muffin's eyes weren't open yet, but he could feel his brothers and sisters crowding around him and everything was good.

Next one, next one, Jane ordered herself as she released Muffin. She reached for the closest hand—and felt the skin under her fingers slither away. Her eyes jerked down and she saw the white bones and tendons of the hand she held. Slowly she looked up at the person's face. She could see pieces of white bone there too.

"Oh, Thomas. Oh, God." Take us someplace happy, she pleaded. An instant later, she was with Thomas, Thomas whole and healthy. He leaned against one of the pine trees on the point, sketching a picture of Tavia. It wasn't very good. But Jane could feel the love. He really did love Tavia.

They were back. The flaming vine in Thomas's mouth disintegrated, and Thomas lay still. Jane knew he was dead even before she forced herself to kneel and check his pulse, and all she could feel was relief.

At least love was the last thing he felt, she told herself as she reached for the next hand, realizing for the first time that she was walking through the flames without being burned. No time to think about it. She worked her way from person to person, gathering strength from their memories—even the one from Matthew Plett, who went back to something like age ten when his dad decided he was old enough for a beer.

Jane's brain throbbed from shifting back and forth in time so often, so fast. But she forced herself to move on to the next person—Billy, the handyman from the hospital. Before she could take his hand, a hideous squawking cry rang out above her. And birds began to hit the earth like giant hailstones.

One of the tree's thin branches of fire swept across the sky. This time Jane saw the lavender threads blacken before she heard the death cries of more birds, then the thuds as they hit the ground. Nothing I'm doing is making a difference, Jane thought. The tree has gotten too much fuel already.

So what are you going to do—sit down and give up? Jane asked herself. To answer her question, she grabbed Billy's hand and went back with him a few years at most. He was down on the beach in the winter, rain coming down. But Billy had his shoes off and his head tilted back, strolling along like it was the most beautiful day ever.

Next, Jane thought as Billy fell to the ground, disconnected from the tree. Free.

She took a step, then froze. "Mom?" she squeaked out, though she knew her mother couldn't hear her. She grabbed her mother's hand, then realized her father stood a few feet closer to the tree.

Jane didn't know if she could do two people at once, but she wanted both her parents free of the evil. Right now. She reached out and grabbed her father with her free hand.

And she heard giggling from the tree above her. Not the tree of hate. One of the big leafy trees on the point. She looked up and saw herself at about five years old sitting in the tree with Elijah. Elijah put one hand over her mouth, trying to shush her, even though he was starting to laugh too.

"I don't think we're ever going to find them," Jane's dad exclaimed loudly from almost directly below little Jane's and Elijah's hiding place.

"Our children are much too clever for us," Jane's mother agreed. She came up behind Jane's dad and wrapped her arms around him. "What will we do if we haven't found them before it gets dark?"

"Here we are!" little Jane yelled.

Jane smiled. She never could stand to hide for more than two seconds.

"There you are!" Her father swung her down from the tree and handed Jane to her mom. Then he grabbed Elijah and held him upside down by the ankles until his face turned red.

"Do you think we should take these two home?" Jane's dad asked her mother.

"Absolutely," Jane's mother answered. "No one could love them as much as we do."

"And no one could love you as much as I do," Jane's dad said softly as he put Elijah's feet back on the ground.

Jane wished she could stay right there for just one more minute. But they were back. She allowed herself one fast look at her parents, lying on the ground, their faces peaceful now that they were free. Then she moved on. And on. And on.

When Jane had disconnected the last person, she sank down onto the ground. It was warm, too warm for such a late fall day. She looked around and realized that the fire on the vines was moving onto the earth. The dirt was beginning to burn.

There's nothing else I can do, Jane thought. She stretched out on the ground, ignoring the heat, and opened her mouth. I hope Seth gets back soon, she thought, then she sighed as one of the lavender threads slid through her lips.

Seth saw the fire long before he reached the tree. He could almost feel blisters rising on his skin as he looked at the blaze.

Was he too late? Was it over? Where was Jane?

He ran faster, his muscles screaming in protest. The ghosts, all those touched by the evil, swooped past him—the old man who had skinned himself, the girl who had been raped by her father, and so many more—moving so quickly they were almost a blur.

"Wait!" Seth yelled. He didn't know what would happen if they just hurled themselves at the flaming tree. "Wait!"

The ghosts moved as one, veering to the left. They joined hands and opened their mouths for a bouquet of lavender cords. What the hell had happened while he'd been gone?

The tree had caught fire, the oily mucus sending out clouds of smoke. But something else had changed too. Across from the tree was a mass of the lavender stuff. It reminded him of seaweed swaying in a current. Except that it was starting to smoke. Any second now the cords were going to burst into flame.

As Seth watched, the lavender cords running out of the ghosts' mouths began to sparkle with droplets of water. The droplets ran together until each lavender cord was coated with a thin stream of water. The water spread until every cord shone with its own rivulet. Not enough to put out the fire. But enough to prevent the cords from being consumed by it.

It's perfectly balanced. The ghosts' energy balanced it. It was like Terry said, all that was left in them was what they had loved, and they were pumping that love into the cords.

A little more power on either side and that would be it, Seth realized. More juice to the tree and the flames would burn everything. More juice to the seaweed—he couldn't help thinking of it that way—and the water would wash everything clean.

One of the tree's yellow-green branches snaked over to Seth. He locked his teeth. The evil wasn't going to feed on him, no way. But the branch simply thinned itself out and slid inside. Seth could feel the oily fire all the way down in his belly as the evil moved around down there, searching.

Images spewed into Seth's mind. There he was, choking down Pop-Tarts. There he was, barfing them up. What kind of loser did that? What kind of loser couldn't deal with life without freakin' Pop-Tarts?

Yeah, Jane could forgive poor little boy Seth for accidentally killing his friend. It was an accident. He didn't mean to kill Terry.

But he didn't accidentally stuff himself full of crap. He didn't accidentally shove his finger down his throat and throw the crap back up. There was something wrong with him. He should chain himself up inside a cave somewhere. Nobody should have to be around him. Especially not Jane.

Seth could feel the branch inside him heating up. Something was flowing through it. Something from him. It was all that crap he was thinking. But he couldn't stop it.

He'd told Jane he wasn't any kind of hero. And he was right. Look at the tree. It was flaring up, flaring up with the fuel Seth was pumping into it. The balance was shifting. The edges of the lavender seaweed had started to blacken.

Stop it, Seth ordered himself. Stop it! But the images kept coming. Seth sitting on the edge of the tub, eating a whole cake, using his hands to shove it into his mouth. Seth pouring Jell-O powder down his gullet, chomping on uncooked spaghetti. Anything he could get his friggin' hands on. What kind of person did that?

Seth felt something tickle his lips. He looked down, his eyes almost crossing, and saw one of the lavender threads slide into his mouth.

Instantly, an image of Jane filled his mind. Jane smiling at him.

He loved her. He'd never been in love before, but that was the only thing this feeling could be. Love. When he was with her, he was the Seth he most wanted to be. He could say anything to her. He could tell her about his scarf-and-barf crap, he knew that now, seeing her face in his mind. He could tell her, and it would be okay. Because she loved him too.

He squeezed his eyes shut, and waited for the counter-attack. For that voice inside him to start saying that there was no way anyone could love Seth if she really knew him. But it didn't come. Because it wasn't true. Jane loved him. She loved him!

Seth felt something else surging out of him. Something new. Not that old self-loathing garbage. Something clean and cold and fresh. It surged out of him, endless, easily putting out the remains of the oily fire in his gut.

He opened his eyes. And saw a fountain of sparkling silvery water erupt from one of the lavender seaweed cords. Was it the cord connected to him? He didn't know. Didn't care.

A moment later, a fountain burst out of another cord. It arced up and out, a geyser of water, splashing down on the oily fire of the tree.

Sizzling and sputtering sounds, like the world's largest bacon strip in the world's largest frying pan, filled the air. Somewhere nearby, another fountain gushed free. Seth laughed as the cold water pelted him, pasting his hair to his head.

"We won!" he shouted. And he'd shifted the balance. It had all come down to him and somehow he hadn't caved.

With an almost human groan the tree collapsed into a pile of ash. And the gushing water from the fountains—dozens of them, hundreds of them—took the ash out into the sea.

It was over. It was truly over.

And Jane's arms were around him.

Epilogue

This was it. The make-or-break moment.

"Ravens! Ravens! Ravens!" Jane shouted until she thought her vocal cords would snap.

Then the chant changed to "McFadden!" and she realized she could yell even louder. Elijah and Tavia sat next to her in the bleachers, shouting almost as loud as she was, except that they had to stop and kiss after practically every syllable.

The chant grew softer but more intense, as Seth took his place at the free throw line. Jane lowered her voice too, her eyes locked on Seth. If he made both the shots, the game was theirs. If not, game over. There wouldn't be time to make the points they needed.

Seth seemed to barely glance at the net. He just let the ball free and—*swish*!

Now it was all down to one last throw.

Jane spared a glance at Seth's parents. Seth's dad was leaning forward, his hands tightly gripped together. Relax, she wanted to tell him. Haven't you been watching all night? Seth's in the zone.

Seth had the ball in his hands. He only took a second to adjust his position, then threw the ball. *Swish!*

Jane leapt to her feet. "Yeah!" she cried.

Andrea Callison shot her a nasty look, but Jane didn't care. She was tired of being invisible. "Yeah!" she yelled again.

"You're wonderful," Jane whispered as she sat back down. She knew that a month ago Seth probably would have choked on one of those shots. At least that's what he'd told her happened at his old school. They'd been telling each other a lot of things. Jane was still amazed at what came pouring out of her when she was with Seth.

"You're wonderful," her brother repeated in a high voice that Jane was sure sounded nothing like hers.

"You were never that good when you were out there," Jane retorted.

"True," Elijah admitted. "In fact, I was told in no uncertain terms that I'm not recruitment material." He gave one of Tavia's braids a tug. "I still want to play next year. But I might run for class president or something too. Round out my high school record. Got to get into a good school."

"You have one in mind?" Tavia asked.

"I'm waiting to see where a certain person is accepted," Elijah answered. "Persons, I should say. Aren't the Olsen twins going to college soon?"

Tavia's reply was drowned out by the massive cheer as

the clock ran out and the Ravens won the game. Vince Pullman and Chad Williams tried to hoist Seth onto their shoulders, but he fought his way down.

Go on, Seth, Jane silently urged him. Enjoy it.

She expected him to walk into the locker room with the rest of the team. Instead, he charged into the bleachers, ignoring the cries of protest and congratulations, and kissed her.

Then he turned to the crowd, accepted their applause with a wide grin, and actually gave a bow. He definitely wouldn't have done that a month ago, Jane thought as Seth sat down next to her.

"So you want to go up to the point?" he whispered in her ear.

At first Jane had thought she'd never want to go to the point again. But she had so many great memories of things that had happened there—her own memories and memories that had become a part of her when she had disconnected the people of her town from the evil that fed on them. Those memories had turned out to be stronger than the darkness she'd experienced on the point.

"I hope you are asking my sister if she wants to go out for an ice cream cone in a well-lit place," Elijah said.

"Your sister makes the calls," Seth answered.

"You can take me for an ice cream cone, Elijah," Tavia chimed in.

"So ice cream or—?" Seth asked, his lips so close to her face that she could feel his warm breath against her ear.

"Raven's Point," Jane told him. She was looking forward to racking up a few new memories. With Seth.